THE CHINESE WAS WIELDING A BULLWHIP...

He raised it as Jessie watched and snapped its tip back, then the braided tip sped forward like a snake and wrapped itself around the throat of the running man. The coolie was unable to stop in time to keep the whip from pulling him to the ground.

A crash of glass exploded from the anteroom. Out of the corner of her eye, Jessie saw Ki land a yard or two from the foreman after his leap through the window. Instead of aiming his whip's cutting blow at the recumbent coolie, the giant switched his aim. The tip swung around. Ki stood directly in its path...

LONE STAR

The Exciting New Western Series from the Creators of Longarm!

WESLEY ELLIS

LONE STAR

IN THE TALL TIMBER

A JOVE BOOK

LONE STAR IN THE TALL TIMBER

A Jove Book / published by arrangement with
the author

PRINTING HISTORY
Jove edition / January 1983

ISBN: 0-515-06232-4

PRINTED IN THE UNITED STATES OF AMERICA

★

Chapter 1

"I'd feel a lot better about this if I knew as much as you do about *ninjutsu,*" Jessica Starbuck told Ki in a low voice.

"You don't have to worry," Ki replied.

He stopped abruptly and Jessie gasped involuntarily when she saw the prone figure of a man stretched across the sidewalk, his head and shoulders propped up on the bottom step of a small house. Ki bent over the man, straightened up, stepped over the prone form, and motioned for Jessie to follow. They continued up the street, Jessie looking back at the sprawled body of the man on the ground.

"Just a sailor sleeping off a spree," Ki told her. He went on, "Tonight we won't need the *ninja* tactics I used yesterday to keep from being noticed. You've seen how people avoid looking at each other in this part of the city."

"I'm not worried," Jessie said. "I just don't want to give the cartel any hint that we've visited what they still think is a secret headquarters."

"They'll never know we were there," Ki assured her. "There's only one guard. We can get past him without being seen, as dark as it is tonight. If the locksmith did a good job, the cartel will never know we've visited them. And when we leave, the fog will be our friend."

Chilling fingers of dense wet fog had begun creeping in from San Francisco Bay even before Jessie and Ki passed the last of the flaring gaslights that advertised the Barbary Coast's palaces of sinful pleasures. Continuing on into the darkness that shrouded the street ahead of them, they kept close to the walls of the buildings, which were a typical waterfront mixture of ship supply stores, quack medical offices, sailors' boardinghouses, small frame dwellings, and bulky warehouses that extended back from the wharves. A few more minutes of walking took them to the sleazy three-story red brick building that was their goal. Across the street from the building, they stopped. A single red pinpoint glowed in the doorway that opened on one side of the structure.

"That's the guard, I'm sure," Ki said. "He'll finish his cigar and then go inside to make his rounds. We'll give him a few minutes to get through with the second floor. While he's on the third floor, we'll have time to reach the office we're after."

"And I hope I'm right about finding what we're looking for there," Jessie said, her eyes fixed on the glowing tip of the cigar in the black frame of the open door across the street. "It's possible that the fire up north was an accident, but when anything bad happens to one of the Starbuck properties, my first reaction is to suspect the cartel."

"So far, you've been right."

"Yes. They've kept us busy since they murdered my father."

Jessie's father, Alex Starbuck, had been ambushed and killed by assassins who were lackeys of the international cartel that, even before his death, had tried ceaselessly to wrest the vast Starbuck holdings away from the man who had singlehandedly created them. Taking over after her father's death, Jessie, with the help of Ki, had been involved in a constant battle against the cartel's aggressions.

When they'd checked into their hotel the previous afternoon, after returning from a trip to Hawaii, where problems

2

at a Starbuck sugar cane plantation had required Jessie's personal attention, a telegram had been waiting for her at the registration desk. The wire was from the bookkeeper of the lumber mill in Baytown, Oregon, which had been one of Alex's first ventures when he began his expansion. The mill had burned in a mysterious fire in which the manager had been killed.

"There hasn't been a fire at that mill since Alex put Tom Buck in charge of it," Jessie had frowned, passing the telegram over to Ki. "Tom was a very careful man. But there's been something wrong up there, Ki. The mill's been losing money for the past two years, which it never did before."

"Could Tom Buck have sold out, Jessie?"

"No. Alex always trusted him. He said Tom was completely loyal."

"Then somebody from outside is responsible."

"Yes. And that can only mean one thing."

Ki nodded soberly. "The cartel, of course."

"Exactly. I've been postponing a visit to Baytown far too long, and even if this won't be quite what I'd planned..." She stopped and reread the telegram.

"This is as close as we've been to Oregon for quite a while, Jessie. Are we going to Baytown, then?"

Jessie made no reply other than a brief nod. She thought for a moment before going on.

"Ki, do you remember the mysterious address we found on that cartel thug who was killed in Colorado? The one who'd come to the mines from San Francisco?"

"Of course," he replied. "It was an address on Jackson Street, just off the Embarcadero."

"This is the first chance we've had to investigate it. I'm sure it's some sort of private headquarters of the cartel, one where they hire the thugs and gunmen they use, the kind of men who'd look out of place going into the cartel's headquarters in the financial district."

3

"And you think there might be some clue in that office about the fire at the Baytown mill?"

"Yes," Jessie answered decisively. "They'd send an arsonist from here, I'm sure."

"It's logical," Ki agreed. "Do you want to look at the place tonight?"

"No. Tomorrow night. My legs feel like we're still on the China clipper."

"Then I'll look at it alone, first. There's plenty of time left for me to do that if I start right now. I'll find out what we might run into. Tomorrow night, we'll go together and make a real investigation."

Ki's knowledge of *ninjutsu,* the art of the "invisible assassins" of old Japan, enabled him to move around busy places without being noticed; thus he had been able to go through the Jackson Street building undetected.

"It has the smell of a cartel headquarters," he'd told Jessie after his preliminary survey. "The first floor's occupied by a store selling sailors' clothes and supplies; it'd make a good cover for the cartel. The upper floors have a separate entrance. There's a big room on the third floor where there are fifteen or twenty cots, and in one of the other rooms on that same floor, there's a kitchen. They look as though they're used only occasionally. There are offices on the second floor. I tried the doors, and they were all locked."

"Perhaps we'd better not bother with it, if it's only used occasionally." Jessie's voice showed her disappointment at seeing what might have been a fruitful lead vanishing. "I'd like to try to get into the cartel's downtown headquarters, but my father had no luck when he tried. In his diary he noted that the place is heavily guarded around the clock, and the lights burn all night."

"Only the top floor of the Jackson Street building doesn't seem to be used regularly, Jessie. The offices on the second

4

floor look like they're busy. And just as I left there, a guard came on duty for the night. The place wouldn't be guarded if those offices didn't have something important in them."

Jessie's face brightened immediately. "We'll go ahead with our plans, then, Ki. It isn't often that we get a chance to get a step or two up on the cartel. If there's anything in those offices that will help us, we'd be fools not to try to find it!"

Across the street, the red dot they'd been watching while they talked arced into the middle of the brick pavement and lay there, slowly fading to invisibility. The black opening of the doorway took on a lighter shade as the door was closed.

Jessie started to cross the street, but Ki put a hand on her arm and stopped her.

"Wait for a minute longer," he said. "The guard checks the lower floor first. We don't want to get to the door until he's gone upstairs. Then, if the locksmith who made keys from the impressions of the locks I made yesterday did a good job, we'll be inside in just a few seconds."

Both Jessie and Ki had worn dark clothing for their foray. Almost invisible in the darkness and the thickening fog, they crossed the street silently. Ki had the door key ready in his hand, and entering the building was the work of a few seconds. They stood for a moment in a narrow hall, breathing the smell of wool and leather from the seamen's store through which the entrance hall ran. The silence inside the narrow corridor was complete.

Ki took two pairs of felt-soled sandals from his pocket and they slid them on over their shoes. When they started for the stairway that was barely visible ahead of them, their feet made only the softest whispering on the rough wooden floor.

Halfway up the stairs they saw the dim glow of the guard's bull's-eye lantern, and heard the clumping of his boots as he mounted the stairs to the top floor. Their eyes were growing used to the blackness now. They stopped and waited until the noise of the footsteps ended and all was dark again, then continued their silent ascent.

At the head of the stairs, Ki led the way to a door at the center of the passage. A square of light, bright only in comparison to the surrounding darkness, marked the upper glass panel of an office door. Straining her eyes, Jessie could read the words painted on the opaque glass: WILSON INVESTMENT COMPANY. She heard the tiny metallic noise made by the key scraping in the lock, then the door swung open and she followed Ki inside.

Dim gray sky-glow, made dimmer by the fog, filtering in around the drawn windowshades, enabled them to see the details of the room in which they now stood. A desk took up most of the center of the office, its surface bare except for an ornate metal inkwell that included a tray in which three or four pens lay. A head-high safe stood in a corner, and a table was placed behind the desk next to the safe. There were a half-dozen chairs strung along the walls in addition to a high-backed, leather-upholstered chair behind the desk.

"It certainly looks bare," Jessie whispered to Ki.

"Yes. Anything worth looking at is probably locked up in the safe." Ki stepped across the room and tried the handles of the safe's door. They refused to yield. He said, "It'd take blasting powder to open this thing."

Jessie had gone to the desk and was opening its drawers. The small drawers on each side of the kneehole were empty. She opened the shallow middle drawer. An envelope, one end torn off, lay in the drawer. She felt inside the envelope. Her fingers encountered a slip of folded paper. She slid it out and moved to the window, but the gray light that showed around the edges of the shade was too dim. She could see

6

only that the half sheet of paper bore a single short line of writing.

"What've you found?" Ki asked.

"I'm not sure. It's a note of some kind, but I can't read it in the dark."

"We'll take it with us, then."

"No," Jessie replied quickly. "If we do that, whoever uses this office will know someone's been here. I'd like to keep our visit a secret, if we can."

"We'll wait until the guard passes on his way downstairs," Ki suggested. "Then I'll strike a match and hold it while you read the note."

"Good. We'll—" Jessie stopped abruptly as the thudding of the guard's footsteps sounded on the stairs.

Freezing into immobility, they waited while the footsteps grew louder. They could trace the man's movements by his steps. They heard him walk slowly down the hall, saw the flicker of the lantern he carried brighten the glass door panel, throwing the painted letters it bore into sharp silhouettes, and then the panel faded to a dimly visible square as the man moved down the hall. Jessie and Ki stood silently until they heard the footsteps returning. They were not prepared for the doorknob of the office to rattle and the door to swing open, flooding the room with light from the guard's bull's-eye lantern.

Jessie had dropped to the floor behind the desk, and Ki had moved to the door at the first rattle of the doorknob. By the time the guard had the door open, Ki was crouched beside it, below the level of the guard's eyes, waiting. As the door swung wide and the man stepped into the room, Ki rose and grasped his throat from behind.

With the skill born of practice, Ki's steel-hard fingers and thumb dug into the plexus of nerves that lay sheltered under the parotis gland below the guard's ear. The instant

7

his grip was locked tightly on the sensitive spot, Ki pulled the man sharply backward and at the same time brought his knee up with precise force into the guard's coccyx. Within seconds the man had slumped down, unconscious. Ki caught the lantern as it fell from his limp hand.

"He'll be out for three or four minutes," he told Jessie. "Here. Hold the note to the lantern and read it."

Jessie stepped to Ki's side and held the paper in the cone of light cast by the lantern's lens. Her voice reflecting the frustration she felt, she told Ki, "I can't read it! It's nothing but gibberish! The note's in code!"

"Copy it, then. You can study it when we get back to the hotel." Ki flashed the lantern toward the desk. "There's ink and some pens, Jessie. But work fast, the guard won't stay unconscious long."

"I need something to write on," Jessie said. She glanced around; a wastebasket that stood beside the desk caught her eye. It was empty except for a wadded-up envelope. She picked it up and quickly smoothed the crumpled paper on the desktop. Then, while Ki held the bull's-eye lantern, she copied the short line of senseless letters from the note to the back of the envelope. Just as she was inscribing the last letter, the guard moaned and started to stir.

"Quick, now!" Ki said. "He'll be coming around soon. I'd put him out again, but if I do it a second time, it could be fatal. He may not be worth much, but there's no point in killing him unless we have to."

Carrying the lantern, Ki lighted their way downstairs. Halfway down the flight of steps, Jessie stopped.

"What's wrong?" Ki asked.

"I did a stupid thing, Ki. I was so interested in that message that I didn't think to look at the postmark on the envelope it was mailed in." She started back up the stairs. "I'm going to go look. It'll only take a moment."

"No, Jessie! It's too dangerous! That guard was beginning to come to before we left. The effect of that *te* hold I used wears off fast."

A moan reaching their ears from the landing above their heads underlined Ki's words. Reluctantly, Jessie let Ki nudge her ahead. They reached the first floor. Ki blew out the lantern and set it inside the door, and he and Jessie stepped out into the street, where, within a moment or two, they were swallowed up by the fog.

They walked briskly along the two deserted blocks of Jackson Street until they reached the Embarcadero, where the lights of the saloons and brothels still gleamed from the side streets. Keeping on the dark side of the wide thoroughfare in front of the wharves, they reached California Street, went up it to Montgomery, and were soon safely in the hotel.

"We'll go to my room," Jessie said as they crossed the wide lobby. "I'll see if I can make any sense out of this note by studying it where I can see what I've written down."

In the room, with the gaslights turned up, Jessie studied the envelope while Ki watched her. After a moment she shrugged and said, "I copied that note in such a hurry that I can barely read what I've written here. Maybe it'll help if I rewrite it on a clean sheet of paper."

Sitting at the small writing desk, she took a sheet of hotel stationery from the drawer and recopied the letters she'd scribbled under pressure in the office. She laid the envelope on which she'd made the original copy on the desktop. Ki picked it up and looked at it curiously. He turned it over and read the address, then glanced at the return address printed in the upper left corner.

"Jessie," he said, "Did Alex ever prove that the Farmers' & Mechanics' Bank was the one the cartel uses here?"

"He didn't succeed in proving it, but he was satisfied that his hunch was right. That's why we use Mr. Crocker's bank now."

9

"This envelope came from the Farmers' & Mechanics' Bank. I suppose the man it's addressed to is the one whose name's on the door of that office, Mr. Gordon Wilson."

"Wilson, yes, that was it, Wilson Investment Company," Jessie replied absently, her eyes still fixed on the sheet of paper.

Her frown deepened as she looked at the three groups of letters she'd transferred from the envelope. Then her frown became a smile and she looked up.

"Ki, thank you!" she exclaimed. "I think you've given me just the clue I needed!"

Ki stepped around to look over Jessie's shoulder. She took a fresh sheet of paper and very carefully printed on it the three groups of letters over which she'd been puzzling:

FECXSAR NSF JMRMWLIH

Jessie then very carefully printed the alphabet below the group of letters. She ran the point of her pen along the line made by the alphabet and stopped when she reached the letter W. Below the W, she wrote A, then printed B under the X, C under the Y, and D below the Z. Moving her pen back to the beginning of the alphabet, Jessie printed E below the letter A, F under B, and swiftly finished out the remaining letters of the alphabet, with Z on the lower line falling under the letter V. Raising her head, she studied the two lines of letters:

ABCDEFGHIJKLMNOPQRSTUVWXYZ

EFGHIJKLMNOPQRSTUVWXYZABCD

"Now we'll see if my guess is right," she told Ki.

"You seem to know what you're doing," he commented. "Which is more than I do."

"This message had to be a very simple substitition cipher, Ki," she explained. "The men sending messages to this Wilson couldn't afford to carry a written key, so it had to be some clue they could carry in their heads, something they couldn't forget. What could be better than the first letter of Wilson's name?"

"You know I haven't studied up on codes and ciphers like you have, Jessie," Ki said. "I don't know what a substitution cipher is."

"One letter substituting for another. The trick in such a short message is to discover the pattern that was used. In this case, it was W."

Running her penpoint along the two lines of the alphabet, Jessie found the correct letters and printed them below the message she'd copied in the office. Ki watched the message take its correct form:

FECXSAR NSF JMRMWLIH

BAYTOWN JOB FINISHED

"I suppose it's simple, when you know what to look for," he said. "It's proved our hunch was right, Jessie. The burning of that lumber mill in Baytown was the work of the cartel."

"Yes. You'd better go down to the desk before you go to your room, Ki. Find out when the first train tomorrow morning leaves for Oregon. We're going to be on it. This is one attack the cartel's going to pay for!"

★

Chapter 2

"That must be the stagecoach station across the street," Jessie said to Ki as they stood with their luggage at their feet on the depot platform in Salem.

Behind them, the Southern Pacific train that had brought them from San Francisco was already sliding out of the depot siding. Jessie and Ki examined their surroundings.

A rutted gravel road paralleled the railroad tracks to the west. Across the road, the square frame building of the stagecoach station and a few stores and warehouses were scattered at random across a treeless slope that descended steeply to the green waters of the Willamette River. Branching off the main road, a narrower one zigzagged down to the tiny ferry slip that stood at the water's edge, and in the slip was a flat-decked, bargelike boat without a cabin, superstructure, or smokestack.

Beyond the tracks to the east, the business section and dwellings of Oregon's capital city made a pattern of neat squares centered roughly on a tall white frame structure which they guessed must be the capitol building. Past the last row of houses the ground began to rise, bathed by the declining sun, a thickly timbered slant cresting in the broken line of a ridge that connected a series of gently rounded green hills and marked the end of the river valley. Except

12

for a wisp of fast-dissipating smoke left by the departing train, the air was crystal clear.

Ki picked up the bags. "We'd better take our luggage over and make sure of the time the stage leaves, then."

"Yes. This is a pretty enough place, but I'd hate to miss the stage and have to wait over until this time tomorrow."

At the stage station, the clerk greeted them with a nod; then, after a frowning glance at the almond-shaped eyes that gave away Ki's Japanese ancestry, he ignored Ki and directed his remarks exclusively to Jessie.

"It'll be a while before the stage can leave, ma'am. Maybe an hour or so. The coach busted a spring leaf on that blamed rough road over the Coast Range, and they're just getting it fixed now. Was I you, I'd go back over to the railroad depot and get a bite to eat while you're waiting. I know it's early for supper, but you'll have plenty of time, and the driver's going to be pushing, so he'll cut short on the supper stop at Rickreall."

"When will we get to Baytown, then?" Jessie asked.

"Sometime around noon tomorrow. It's a good sixty miles, and the road's crookeder'n a gopher snake."

"In that case, we'd better take the man's advice," Jessie told Ki, who nodded. She asked the clerk, "Our luggage will be safe here, I suppose?"

"Sure will. I'll keep an eye on it myself."

Their snack at the depot proved a pleasant surprise: thin slices of baked salmon arranged in layers that rose a full inch above a thick, crusty slice of freshly baked bread. When they got back to the depot, the stage was drawn up in front of the building, the driver just checking the harness buckles.

"We'll be pulling out right away," he told them. "So if you folks want to put your luggage in the boot..."

"I'll take care of it," Ki said quickly.

Jessie looked at the stagecoach. It was drawn by two

13

horses instead of the four that made up a stagecoach team on the prairie and in the Rocky Mountains. The coach was much narrower in the body than the roomy Concord-type coaches to which she'd grown accustomed in the flatlands farther east, and the body was quite a bit shorter, with the driver's seat mounted on top of the vehicle instead of midway between the top and the bed. The wheels were closer together, to give it a shorter turning radius. While she was still examining the coach, Ki came out with their bags and put them in the abbreviated boot.

"I suppose we might as well get in," he told Jessie. "The driver was talking with the clerk when I went in, and I heard him say he was finally ready to start."

They were settling into their seats in the stage when the driver came out of the depot, glanced inside, nodded, and swung up into his seat. The iron tires crunched into the gravel and the stage rolled slowly down the slope to the ferry slip.

Ki settled back against the thinly padded seat. "It's going to be close quarters," he remarked. "But we don't have very far to go. You said you've visited the Baytown mill before, Jessie. What kind of trip is it from where we are now?"

"I couldn't say, Ki. The only time I was here before, with Alex, we didn't travel overland. We came on the *Silver Queen*. If I remember correctly, there wasn't even a stagecoach operating then, because the Southern Pacific was still building north."

"This will be as new to you as it is to me, then."

"Yes. But from what I've heard, the Coast Range that we'll be going over is just about as rugged as the Rockies, even if it's not as high."

"Well, at least we'll be comforatble. Even though it has four seats, this coach really wasn't made to carry four."

From outside, they heard the driver shout to the horses, and the coach creaked to a halt at the ferry slip. The driver stuck his head in the windowed top of the door and said, "You might as well just keep your seats. It only takes a few minutes to get across on the ferry."

Ki leaned out and watched as the driver led the team down to the ferry slip and onto the waiting boat. The ferryboat was very little wider than the stagecoach, and Ki guessed that at best it could handle no more than two wagons. He was just getting ready to settle back into his seat when a surrey careened down the road and the driver reined in.

There were two passengers in the surrey, a man and a woman. The woman alighted and joined the driver in helping the male passenger to the ground. Ki understood why when he saw her reach into the surrey and hand the man a crutch before turning back to wrestle a large wooden crate from its bed. Meanwhile, the driver of the surrey had run to the ferry landing and was talking to the stagecoach driver.

"What on earth is happening, Ki?" Jessie asked.

Over his shoulder, he answered, "It looks like I was wrong when I said we wouldn't be too crowded. I gather that two late passengers have just arrived, so we'll have company on our trip, after all. A man and a woman. They got here just in time."

In a moment, the driver flung open the door of the coach. "Got a couple more passengers," he announced. "Sorry to hold things up, but it won't take more'n a minute to get 'em on."

Beyond the driver, Jessie and Ki could see the late arrivals now. The man, wearing a pearl-gray suit with a long-cut coat, was well along in his middle years. He had a ruddy face and a fringe of short-trimmed beard. He was leaning on a crutch, and when she looked closer, Jessie saw that one of his legs was in a cast. The woman was young; Jessie guessed from her quick, easy manner of walking that she could not be past her middle twenties. She carried the ship-

15

ping crate cradled in her arms, and the crate hid her figure. A wide-brimmed hat shaded her face, but Jessie got an impression of dark eyes and full, pouting lips.

"I'll make room in the boot for your box, Miss Darcy," the stagecoach driver said.

"You most certainly will not!" the girl said quickly. "This box is going to ride inside, on the seat. It's full of glass plates, and I'm not going to risk having any broken after the trouble I took having them shipped here from San Francisco!"

"There just ain't room," the driver protested. "Anyways, your box ain't going to get bounced around no more in the boot than it will inside the coach."

"You know better than that, Webb," the man said. "Now, why don't you just fix things up the way Darcy wants them?"

"Can't do it, Mr. Stone," the driver replied, shaking his head. "You can see I got two passengers aboard already."

"Well, you'd better figure out a way to do it," Stone said. "I've got to have room to rest my leg on the seat across from where I'll be sitting. I can't fold it easily, and I certainly won't be comfortable if I have to put it on the coach floor."

"Dagnabbit, Mr. Stone—" the driver began.

Stone pushed the man aside and hobbled up to peer inside the coach. He gazed at Jessie for a moment and touched his hatbrim with his forefinger before turning his attention to Ki.

"Here, you!" he snapped. "You, Chinaman! Hop out and ride up with the driver! You chinks aren't entitled to take up room that we Americans need, anyhow."

Ki flicked a quick glance at Jessie. Her lips were compressed into a thin angry line. She leaned forward and spoke to Stone across Ki's chest.

"This gentleman is not Chinese, Mr., uh, Stone, is it? And in any case—"

16

Ki interrupted her. "It's all right, Jessie. I don't mind riding outside with the driver. Our luggage fills up the boot, and Mr. Stone needs the seat to rest his leg on. Besides, it'd be a shame if the lady's plates got broken."

Jessie started to continue her protest, but Ki stopped her with a headshake. He got out of the coach and took the crate from the girl's arms.

"Well now, that's better," Stone grunted as Ki put the heavy wooden box on the seat beside Jessie. "Get in, Darcy. We don't want to hold Webb up any longer than necessary."

With a smile and a nod of thanks to Ki, the girl got into the coach. It took the combined efforts of the driver and Ki to get Stone aboard, to lift his stiff leg up to rest his foot on the seat, and then to find a place for his crutch.

"All right, folks, if everybody's satisfied, we'll get moving," Webb said. "I'll try not to jounce you, Mr. Stone, but you know what the road's like after we get past Rickreall."

"I'll manage, Webb," Stone replied gruffly. "Just get us started. We'll be late enough getting to Baytown as it is."

Slamming the coach door, the driver led the team onto the ferry. Ki swung up on the seat to give the ferry crew room to handle the capstan that revolved the oversized wooden cylinder which engaged a steel cable to pull the boat across the river.

There were four men in the crew, and when the boat got far enough from shore to catch the full force of the Willamette's current, Webb, the stagecoach driver, added his muscles to theirs. The thick cable, looped around the huge wooden cylinder that hung on one side of the boat like a sidewheeler's paddle, turned slowly as the current drove the boat against the cable, but the boat continued to forge ahead.

Once the middle section of roiling green water was behind them, and the ferry entered the swirling eddies of the west bank, it moved faster, and was soon safely in its slip. With a wave to the crew, Webb mounted the high seat beside Ki, and the coach pulled off the boat and onto the twin ruts of a dirt road that wound with no apparent purpose toward the forested humps of the Coast Range, which loomed against the sky ahead.

"Didn't have no chance to say this before, mister," Webb told Ki as he settled back and let the horses set their own pace across the stretch that lay between the river and the foothills, "but I'm grateful you didn't make no fuss about letting Eli Stone have his way, back there."

"It cost me nothing," Ki shrugged. "False pride is a thing I gave up long ago."

"Well, Eli thinks he's a lot more important than he is, I guess. But he's pretty much used to folks doing what he wants 'em to." Webb looked at Ki from the corners of his eyes. "You know, for a chink, you talk pretty good American."

"I am not Chinese," Ki replied. "My mother was Japanese, my father an American."

"Well now. I don't recall I ever met no Japs before, but there's plenty of Chineses hereabouts. See, the railroad brought a whole mess of 'em over when they was building grade to the south, over the Sierras, then they moved a bunch of 'em up thisaway when they pushed the rails north from Californy."

"I have heard of that," Ki nodded. Then, half questioning, half stating, he added, "And when the railroad was completed, and the Chinese had no more work, they stayed here."

"That's about the size of it," Webb agreed. "They're right good workers, and most of 'em manages to keep busy, I'll give 'em that. But I guess it's just as good there won't be no more coming over here. We got enough now."

"You say there will be no more coming over, which must mean across the ocean from China. Did Oregon pass the

18

same kind of Chinese Exclusion Act that California did?" Ki frowned.

"Yep. Washington State did, too. And it looks like the Federals is about to do the same. No use building a dike unless you got both ends tight agin the bank."

A tricky series of curves loomed in the rutted trace in front of them as the ruts zigzagged up a steep incline. Webb took up the slack in the reins and fell silent as he devoted his full attention to the team, leaving Ki to watch the scenery.

Trees lined the ridge and stretched beyond it to the higher rise of the Coast Range foothills. Most of the trees were fir, growing high and straight, but there were some low-growing cedars among them, and a few trees with a strange-hued bark that was a mixture of lavender and tan, which Ki could not identify. There was little grass on the ground, but everywhere Ki looked it was covered with profusely billowing growth of broad-leafed vines.

Ki pulled his hat down to shade his eyes against the declining sun and watched the slopes ahead seem to rise higher, their sides now becoming dark as the sunshine left them. The road was becoming steadily rougher and more winding, and after his first burst of conversation Webb did not seem inclined to talk. The stagecoach was entering the edge of timbered land now, and Ki pulled his hat further down on his forehead as the steadily rising ground tilted the vehicle upward and allowed the sun to strike his face. He wondered how Jessie was doing with the passengers inside the coach.

Jessie had remained coolly silent after Stone's insulting remarks to Ki. She stared out the window, ignoring the pair in the seat across, even though her knees brushed against those of Darcy Stone each time their bodies swung to compensate for the swaying of the stage as it reached the winding road through the timber. They'd been riding for almost an hour in the strained, silent atmosphere when the coach made a more pronounced lurch than usual and the knees of the two women collided forcefully.

"Oh, I'm sorry!" Darcy Stone exclaimed. "I should have been more careful."

"It wasn't your fault," Jessie said, her voice coolly detached. "Think nothing of it."

Darcy sat in silence for a moment, then said, "I'm sorry if my father's remark to your servant made you angry, but he didn't mean anything by it. We're really not used to strangers, living in the isolated place we do, and our neighbors all realize that his bark is much worse than his bite."

Jessica could not resist replying, "Ki is not my servant, nor is he Chinese, as your father assumed. We work together as friends. As for his ancestry, his mother was Japanese and his father an American."

"I'm sure Father wouldn't have been so—" Darcy began, but Stone interrupted her.

"I'll do my own apologizing, Darcy," he said, and turned to face Jessica. She did not return the gesture by facing him, but kept her eyes fixed on the battered wooden panel of the coach's inner wall, between the heads of Stone and his daughter. Stone ignored Jessica's stony expression and went on, "I hope you'll pardon me for speaking as I did at the ferry, Miss—or is it Mrs.?"

"Miss," Jessie answered icily. "And my name is Jessica Starbuck."

"Miss Starbuck," Stone went on, "I'm sorry my abrupt manners offended you." He stopped short, and a frown formed on his ruddy features. "Starbuck. You wouldn't by any chance be related to the Starbuck who owns the lumber mill in Baytown, would you?"

"I *am* the Starbuck who owns the lumber mill in Baytown, Mr. Stone," Jessie replied.

Stone's jaw dropped. He blurted, "The hell you say," then came to an abrupt stop and said, "That's something else I guess I'd better add to my apology. I don't normally cuss in front of ladies, it just slipped out."

"I've heard the word before, Mr. Stone," Jessie told him, her voice still chilly. "It doesn't offend me nearly as much as the attitude you displayed earlier."

"Well, I'm afraid I'm a bit crankier than usual today," Stone told her. "My leg was giving me fits right at the time I got out of that surrey, and I spoke without thinking. But I do hope you'll accept my apology as sincere."

In spite of her residual anger, Jessie found her feelings about Stone changing. Belated as it was, his apology seemed honest, and Jessie had encountered the attitude he'd displayed toward Ki in too many other places not to know that it was fairly common. She decided that he was telling the truth about his injured leg affecting his temper, and allowed her face to relax.

Darcy said, "Father didn't think to include an introduction with his apology, Miss Starbuck, but of course you heard our names back at the ferry slip."

"I heard them, but that's about as far as it went. Is Baytown your home, Miss Stone?"

Stone answered before Darcy could speak. "It is, Miss Starbuck. I own the newspaper there, the *Baytown Gazette*, and Darcy not only writes a number of the stories, but she helps me get it on the press and distributed each week."

"And I'm also Father's housekeeper, since mother died three years ago," Darcy put in.

"It sounds to me as if you both have your hands full," Jessie commented.

"We do. The past two or three weeks, after this damned—I apologize again, Miss Starbuck," Stone said. When Jessie waved a hand to indicate that no apology was needed this time, he continued, "These last two weeks have

21

been busier than usual. I had to go to Salem to get this leg of mine attended to properly. Our local doctor said I'd be better off having it done there. So Darcy's been doing my work as well as hers."

"We didn't miss an issue, though," Darcy said proudly. "It wasn't easy, with father away, but it came out on time. And if you don't mind my bragging a bit, the paper looked almost as good as it does when Father's there to do the layout and all the rest of it, even if we did only have four pages instead of eight."

Looking at Darcy now, Stone said, "We're going to have to get used to a four-page paper as long as things are the way they are right now in Baytown, Darcy. But I've mentioned that before, and there's no point in boring Miss Starbuck with our problems."

"I'm not sure I'd be bored with your problems, Mr. Stone," Jessie said. "Not if what is happening in Baytown has a connection with the fire that destroyed my lumber mill."

"Of course it does," Stone replied. "The mill hires more men than all the stores and other businesses in Baytown combined. We're all waiting to find out what's going to happen, but it's taken a long time."

"That's my fault, Mr. Stone," Jessie told him. "But it's not been because I don't care about the mill or about your town. I just happened to be in Hawaii when the mill burned, and I'm on my way to Baytown right now to look the situation over and see what I must do."

"I take that to mean you haven't decided whether you'll rebuild the mill or close it down," Stone frowned.

"From the reports I've had of the fire, there's not much of anything to close down," Jessie replied.

"Well, that's true." Darcy nodded. "All that's left is a good-sized pile of ashes."

"So I'm sure you'll understand—" Jessie began, but before she could go on, a shot barked loudly outside the stage, and the coach rocked to a sudden stop with a rasping of its brakes and a rattle of gravel under the sliding wheels.

Facing forward as she was, Jessie could look out the window more easily than either Stone or Darcy. She leaned forward and craned her neck out the window. The narrow road in front of the stage was blocked by three men on horseback. They had bandannas draped over the bottoms of their faces, and the revolvers in their hands were threatening Webb and Ki.

Jessie pulled her head back inside. "We'll have to continue our conversation later," she told her companions coolly. "It appears that the stagecoach has just been held up."

★

Chapter 3

"All right, everybody outta the coach!" one of the robbers called. The red bandanna covering his face muffled his voice, but did not hide the determination behind his rough command. "You two on the seat, get your hands up high and set still, unless you want your heads blowed off!"

"Damn it, I can't get out!" Stone growled. "At least not by myself!"

"Perhaps you won't have to," Jessie said.

She kept her voice from reflecting the anger she felt at being caught unarmed. Thinking the trip was routine and that she'd be traveling with Ki through civilized country, she'd left her custom-built Colt in her luggage.

Leaning out the window again, she called, "One of the passengers in here can't get out. He has a crippled leg."

"How many of you inside there?" the man asked.

"Three. Two of us are women."

"Men or women, don't make no difference! Get out and leave the door open so I can look inside."

Darcy whispered, "Don't you think we'd better do what they say, Miss Starbuck? That man sounds downright mean!"

"I'm sure he is," Jessie replied. "And you're right, we'd better get out. I'll go first, you follow me. Remember to leave the door open, as he told us to."

24

Jessie stepped out of the coach. The folding stirrup-step that was hinged to the coach's bottom at the center of its door had not been dropped, and the step was unexpectedly long. She staggered and almost fell, but regained her balance just in time to see Darcy make the same mistake of misjudging the distance to the ground. Darcy fell forward with a flurry of skirts and petticoats that left her legs bare to mid-thigh and exposed her ruffled bloomers.

"Gawdamighty!" one of the bandits gasped. "Look at that woman showing her ass!"

"Whaddaya think I'm looking at?" the man beside him asked, his eyes also glued on Darcy's bared legs.

Both men nudged their horses forward to get a closer look, forgetting Webb and Ki.

Until the third bandit spoke, the leader of the trio had been careful to cover Webb and Ki with his revolver and to keep his eyes fixed on them. Now, hearing his companions' comment, the leader turned to look at Darcy. His move gave Ki the opportunity he'd been hoping for. He snapped his right arm down and a *shuriken* slid into his hand from the sheath strapped to his forearm. Ki's arm and hand were a single fluid blur of motion as he sent the *shuriken* whirling to the target he'd chosen, the throat of the outlaw leader.

Streaking through the air in a silent spinning flash of silvery steel, the *shuriken* buried itself in the leader's throat. Its razor-sharp edges cut through the thin cloth of the bandanna and found flesh. The blade penetrated deeply enough to sever the man's jugular vein and windpipe.

With a strangling, bubbling gasp, the outlaw leader let his gun fall and clawed at his throat. His companions had not been watching either their prisoners or their leader, but had let their horses carry them up to the stagecoach. Although the men did not realize it, they were now within Ki's reach.

Their eyes were fixed on their leader after he'd dropped

25

his gun and brought his hands up to his throat to tear away the star-shaped wafer of steel that was draining his lifeblood and depriving him of breath.

They had been watching Darcy when Ki sent the *shuriken* on its mission of death, and were paying no attention to Ki now as they stared at their leader, who was tearing at his throat, his hands dripping with the blood that was spurting around the edges of the *shuriken*. They did not at once connect his strange behavior with the men on the stagecoach seat, for this was the first time they'd encountered such a thing.

When they did make the connection in their minds, it was too late. Their slow advance had placed them in the position that Ki had been anticipating in the few seconds that had passed since he'd thrown the *shuriken*. He brought his knees up to his chest and set his feet solidly on the stagecoach seat. Just as the two outlaws reached the corner of the stagecoach, he launched his attack.

With a tremendous thrust of his powerfully muscled legs, Ki propelled himself into the air. The two outlaws saw him start up from the seat and fired almost as he sprang, but their reflexes weren't quite fast enough. The slugs from their guns whistled through thin air.

His leap placed him between the two outlaws as his momentum diminished and he began to arc to the ground. While still in midair, Ki stabbed into the nearest bandit's Adam's apple with his stiffened toes. A split second later, as his trajectory brought his hands within reach of the second man, he jabbed with rigidly held fingers into the soft, vulnerable spot below the outlaw's jaw.

Twisting his body in midair, Ki landed lightly on his feet, facing the two men he'd just struck, ready to make a second attack if his first had been ineffectual.

It had not been. The outlaw who'd received the kick had let his pistol drop to the ground and was tottering back and

26

forth in his saddle as he clasped his hands around his paralyzed vocal cords and fought for breath. The second man, his left side temporarily paralyzed, was flailing his right arm around, trying to hold himself erect. His weapon flew from his wildly gyrating hand and bounced off the side of the stagecoach. Webb had been frozen in his seat, gaping at Ki and the outlaws, but the thud of the pistol on the coach brought him back to realization of what was happening. He dropped to the ground and retrieved the fallen revolver. Picking it up, he took quick aim at the man who'd dropped the gun and sent a bullet into his heart. The bandit fell limply from his saddle.

"Hold your fire, Webb!" Ki shouted as the stagecoach driver swiveled to take aim at the second outlaw. "I want him alive!"

Both Ki and Webb turned away from the disabled man to look at the leader. They were just in time to see his torso lurch forward and slide sideways from his saddle. One booted foot was still engaged in his stirrup, and as the man slid to the ground, the stirrup held that foot above the saddle. The leader's shoulders landed on the ground, and he lay with his head thrown back, his hat rolling away from his head. Above the line of the masking bandanna, his eyes were glazing in death.

Jessie was accustomed to reacting quickly to Ki's attacks. She had been expecting the flashing streak of steel and saw the *shuriken* bury itself in the outlaw leader's throat. When the man dropped his gun, Jessie started for it.

She moved with calm assurance, knowing that Ki had already planned some kind of attack to take the two remaining bandits out of action. While Ki was still in midair, Jessie picked up the leader's weapon. She was leveling it at the two remaining members of the trio at the moment Webb's shot cut one of them down.

When Ki shouted at Webb, Jessie ran up to the single

27

outlaw who was still mounted and dragged him off his horse—no hard task, since he was already slipping from his saddle. Planting the cold muzzle of the pistol on the man's forehead, Jessie locked his half-glazed eyes with hers.

"Move an inch and you're a dead man," she said coldly. The bandit tried to answer, but only a strangled gurgle came from his lips. Ki came up and ripped the bandanna from the man's face. Holding the big handkerchief by its ends, he flipped the loose triangular corner around to form a makeshift binding, and secured the surviving bandit's wrists behind his back.

Ki had moved so swiftly in his triple attack that when he stood up after tying the outlaw's wrists, Darcy was just getting to her feet. She gaped at the sight that met her eyes—all three outlaws on the ground, two of them dead, Jessie holding one of their guns and Webb the other, and Ki standing unruffled as he rose from binding the third outlaw.

"What—what on earth happened?" Darcy asked of nobody in particular, her eyes moving from one fallen man to the other. "I only heard one shot, but two of them look like they're dead."

"They are," Jessie said unemotionally. "Webb shot one of them. Ki killed the other with a throwing blade."

"A throwing blade?" Darcy frowned. "I never—"

"It's too complicated to explain now," Jessie told her. "I'm sure Ki will be glad to tell you about it later."

From the stagecoach, Eli Stone called, "What in hell's going on out there? Will somebody come tell me, or help me out of this damn coach so I can see for myself?"

Raising her voice, Darcy replied, "I'm coming."

She ran to open the door of the stage on the side where Stone was sitting, and before anyone could move to help her, she had her father standing beside her on the ground and was handing him his crutch. Stone hobbled over to the

28

area where the others stood beside the dead outlaws. He looked at the three downed men, and his eyes bulged.

"Will somebody tell me what happened to those men?" he asked. "I never have seen a thing like this before!"

Before anyone could reply, Jessie said briskly, "Instead of standing here talking, don't you think it would be better if we got ready to travel again? We can talk while we're in the stagecoach, and the more time we have on the road before dark, the sooner this trip will be over."

Webb spoke up quickly to second Jessie's suggestion. "The lady's right. We're just barely started. We can drop these dead ones off at Rickreall and let the town marshal there bury 'em, and haul the other one back to Salem and toss him in jail. You folks have got all the rest of the way to Baytown to chew over how one feller without no gun could do so much damage to three pistol-toting holdup men."

Jessie took command with equal speed. She said, "Come on, Mr. Stone. You've seen all there is to see. You'll remember it well enough to write a newspaper story about it."

Darcy said promptly, "Father's not going to write the story, Miss Starbuck. I am."

"You can settle that between you," Jessie told her. "Right now, I'd like for you to help me get your father back into the stagecoach."

Ki came up and said to Webb, "Come on, I'll give you a hand getting the two dead ones on a horse. We can tie the feet of the one who's still alive under one of the other horses and I'll ride the third horse and keep an eye on him."

"Wait a minute," Stone protested. He hobbled up and stood in front of Ki. "I want you to ride inside with us. I want to find out how you went about all this."

"I'm sorry, Mr. Stone," Ki replied. "As you made clear when we left Salem, the coach is too crowded with four people in it, your leg being in the condition it is."

"Well, I was wrong," Stone replied gruffly. "I've already apologized to Miss Starbuck for what I said before, and I'll repeat it to you."

"I accept your apology," Ki said. "But the fact is that the coach is too small, and I prefer to ride with the prisoner over there. I think I can persuade him to do some talking that might help the officials later on."

For a moment, Ki thought that Stone was going to flare up in anger again, but the newspaper editor was no fool in spite of his blustering ways. He nodded and said calmly enough, "I'll have to admit you're right. But after we get rid of the bodies and the prisoner at Rickreall, maybe you'll feel like riding inside the rest of the way, so we can talk."

"Let's talk about that when we get there," Ki replied. "I promised to help Webb get us ready to travel, and I'd better go do that right now."

Stone had little choice but to nod agreement. He started to hobble toward the coach, but stopped and turned when Ki called to him, "I forgot to ask you, Mr. Stone. Have you ever seen any of these three men around Baytown?"

Stone shook his head. "No. That was the first thing I looked to see. They're all three strangers to me."

"Thank you. We'll talk again in Rickreall."

Ki and Webb spent less than a quarter of an hour lashing the bodies across the back of one of the horses and tying the feet of the survivor under the belly of his horse. Holding the lead rope he'd tied to the animal's reins, Ki swung into the saddle of the third horse and waved to Webb, who climbed up to the stagecoach seat. He geed the team, and the stage rolled ahead, its wheels in the ruts that led through the trees to Rickreall, the horse carrying the bodies of the dead outlaws hitched to the flap that covered the coach's boot.

Ki waited until the stage had a short lead, and nudged his own horse into motion. He waited until the animals had found the gait that suited them best, and pulled the lead rope to bring the outlaw's horse alongside him. Ki had not gagged the man, but he had replaced with a short length of rope the bandanna he'd used to bind his wrists, and had secured the rope to the outlaw's saddlehorn so he could ride more easily. The outlaw looked apprehensively at Ki as his horse came abreast, but he said nothing.

Ki looked at him coldly for a moment before saying, "Suppose you tell me your name. And while you're talking, I'd like the names of those men hanging over that horse ahead of us."

For a moment the man's throat worked convulsively as he tried to make his battered larynx function again, and when he succeeded, his voice came out in a sort of hoarse wheeze.

"Name's Bender," he rasped. "Them two dead ones is Sam Grady—he's the one that got his guzzle cut open— and the other one's name is Anse. I never did know the rest of it."

"You sound like the three of you just got together," Ki suggested. "Have you been working together long?"

"No." The outlaw started to shake his head, but winced and held himself still when his movement sent pains stabbing into his bruised throat. "Dammit, what're you asking all these questions for? I don't think I got a mind to tell you nothing. You got no right to go pushing and prying into a man's private affairs."

Ki sat silent for a moment, studying the man riding beside him. He wore the flannel shirt and cotton duck jeans that most cowhands favored, and his battered hat was creased Californian-style. He was long past the prime of youth. Deep creases ran from his nose to the corners of his crooked lips, and there were crinkled patches at the outer corners of his eyes. He was overdue for a shave by about a week, and the dust ground into the stubble showed Ki his personal

31

habits did not include regular bathing or even washing.

"You'd better be glad you're still alive to answer a few questions," Ki said. He motioned toward the bodies on the horse following the stagecoach. "If I hadn't stopped the driver from shooting you, you'd be hanging over a horse like your friends up there."

Bender gazed at the two bodies for a silent, thoughtful moment, then said, "All right. What do you want to know?"

"Start with the question I just asked you. Have the three of you been together long?"

"No. This was our first job."

"Whose idea was it? Grady's? Yours? Anse's?"

"Hell, it wasn't nobody's." Bender's voice was returning to normal now, though he still wheezed as he spoke. "We was all three setting in a saloon back at Salem—"

"Wait a minute," Ki interrupted. "What brought you to Salem?"

"I can't answer for them other two, but I just been drifting since I got give my time a month ago by old Henry Miller's foreman down at Gustine, in California. I guess you must've heard about Henry Miller?"

Ki nodded. He knew the legendary West Coast cattleman by reputation, and, like everyone in the West connected with ranching, had heard it said that a herd of Miller's cattle could be driven from the Canadian border to Mexico and stop every night on Miller land.

"Go on," he told Bender. "You got fired from your job and drifted. How'd you meet Grady and Anse?"

"Just like I met up with a lot of other fellers. We run into each other a few times in different saloons, and pretty soon we taken to joining up, just for company."

"All right, go ahead," Ki said.

"Well, a night or two ago, all of us was feeling pretty good. We got to bragging a little about how mean we was,

32

the tough outfits we'd rode with other places, and the first thing we knowed, we was talking about holding somebody up. You know how it is."

"No, I don't. Suppose you tell me."

"Well, shit, whoever'd paid for the last round said it was time for one of the other ones to buy. I think it was Anse said that. And I didn't have two dimes to rub together. Turned out Grady didn't neither."

"So you decided to rob the stage?"

"Not right off. We jawed about none of us not even having enough cash for another round. Somebody said we'd hafta scrape up some money, and I don't rightly recollect who it was got us started talking about robbing. We talked about a bank job first, but figured we didn't have enough men for that."

"Who had the idea of holding up the stage?"

"It must've been Grady, I guess. Anyhow, it was him wound up bossing the job."

"How did the three of you happen to get together?" Ki asked. "Did somebody arrange for you to meet in that saloon?"

Bender stared at him, a puzzled frown on his unshaven face. "Who'd fix it up for us to get together? What're you gettin' at, mister? You think we're with a gang or somethin' like that?"

"I'm trying to find that out," Ki replied. "Are you?"

"Why, hell, no! There was just the three of us, like I told you. We'd all of us been around Salem two or three days, just stopped to rest from drifting, it turned out after we got to talking together. And the rest of it happened like I said."

Ki nodded. The man's story hung together. He was satisfied now that the stage holdup had not been arranged by the cartel as an attack on Jessie. Bender's words had the

33

ring of truth, and his surprise at the suggestion that he and his companions might be part of a larger gang had been genuine enough.

"All right," Ki said. "I guess that's all I need to know."

"There's somethin' I'd sure as hell like to know," Bender said. "How'd you manage all them tricks you pulled on us? Why, damn it, we didn't know whether you was comin' or goin'!"

"It would take more time than I have to try to tell you that," Ki replied. "You'll just have to keep wondering."

"Maybe there's somethin' you can tell me quick, then."

"Go ahead. What is it?"

"What's gonna happen to me?"

"We'll hand you over to the marshal at that little town up ahead. He'll arrange for you to stand trial. If you're lucky, you won't spend more than a year or two behind bars."

Bender grunted. "A year or two. Damned if I don't think I got the shitty end of the stick. Way I feel now, I'd almost rather be draped over a saddle up there, along with Sam and Anse."

"You might think so now," Ki said, surprised to discover that he actually felt some sympathy for the would-be robber. "But you'll change your mind. A year or two in jail, and you'll be out in the sunshine again. Your two friends up ahead will be underground forever, and forever is a very long time."

★

Chapter 4

In the coach, Eli Stone was questioning Jessie about Ki, and getting what the newspaperman considered inadequate answers.

"You say this man Ki is the son of an American man and a Japanese woman, Miss Starbuck. What sort of man? What kind of woman?" he asked.

Jessie was still nurturing a residue of anger because of the earlier treatment Stone had given Ki. She had no wish to get into an involved discussion with him on the subject. She chose her words carefully to make them the literal truth and at the same time to close the door to any further discussion.

"I can't tell you that, Mr. Stone," she said. "I'm sure my father knew, but he never did give me the complete story before he was killed. And I don't discuss his parentage with Ki."

"And this Ki doesn't ever talk about his folks?"

"No. It's a topic he seems to want to avoid. Since he doesn't bring up the subject, I don't ask him any questions."

Jessie carefully avoided mentioning that Ki's bitterness that the attitude of the Japanese nobility, still a closed and feudal-minded group, had caused him to come to the United States. Nor did she say anything about the almost fatherly attitude that Alex Starbuck had felt for Ki.

"How about all those fighting tricks he used to wipe out three men in as many minutes, without a gun?" Stone asked. "You must know a lot about them too, being around him so much."

Smiling, Jessie shook her head. "The Japanese have their own way of fighting. We call it dirty tricks, because they don't stand toe-to-toe and slug with their fists. It's really a very scientific method of fighting, and it takes many years of study and practice to master it as Ki has. And I certainly don't know enough about it to tell you much. That's something else you'll have to find out from Ki himself."

Darcy had taken little part in the conversation between her father and Jessie. Now she asked, "Has Ki taught you any of his fighting tricks, Miss Starbuck?"

"A few of the simple ones. But I don't take the time to practice as Ki does."

Darcy observed thoughtfully, "Ki must be very strong and keep himself in good shape, to do the things he did to those outlaws. I don't think I'd be able to, any more than you are."

As Jessie hoped he would, Stone had grown more frustrated with each of Jessie's replies, and now he shifted the topic of discussion. "I get the idea you're planning to stay in Baytown a while."

"As long as it takes me to find out why the Starbuck mill burned and to decide whether or not it'll be rebuilt."

"How much do you really know about that mill, and about Baytown, Miss Starbuck?" Stone asked. "I've owned the newspaper there for a long time, and I don't remember that you've ever been there before."

"If you're suggesting that I wouldn't know how to operate the mill myself, Mr. Stone, you're right, I wouldn't. That doesn't mean I'm not interested in its success. And, yes,

I have been to Baytown, though it was a number of years before my father was murdered. Truthfully, I don't remember much about the town."

"Well, the only really important thing for you to know is that the Starbuck mill was the biggest business in Baytown and just about its only regular payroll."

"Surely there are other businesses there!" Jessie protested.

"Retail stores and mill supply houses, yes. But nothing that keeps any sizable number of men at work. The mill's got jobs even when the woods close down."

"What do you mean, 'when the woods close down'?" Jessie frowned. "How on earth can you close down a forest?"

"Logging's not a year-round job," Stone explained. "When the brush and foliage get dry in midsummer, logging stops until the rainy season begins in the fall. But by the time the logging ends, the mill has built up a stockpile of logs to keep it running right on through summer."

"Everybody depends on the mill," Darcy added. "If you just walk away from it and don't rebuild it, you'll put loggers and teamsters and clerks in stores and, well, just about everybody else out of work. Including the *Gazette*. If we can't sell ads to the retail stores, we can't keep operating either."

"I can understand that," Jessie said quietly. "And I can understand why you feel you're entitled to get some kind of assurance from me about the mill's future."

"Don't you think the people in Baytown should know whether it's got a future or not?" Stone demanded.

"Of course I do!" Jessie retorted. "I don't blame you for being impatient because I can't give you a quick yes or no."

"Why don't you give us one or the other, then, Miss Starbuck?" Darcy asked.

"Because I have to make up my mind on the basis of confidential information that I'm not sure I want to share with you."

Darcy turned and looked at her father, her eyebrows raised. He turned down the corners of his mouth, not in a scowl, but in a manner that answered Darcy's unspoken question with a question of his own. Jessie recognized the exchange instantly. The Stones shared the same kind of silent father-daughter communication that had existed between herself and Alex. Many times, they'd resolved problems after two or three such looks, without either of them having said a word. She waited to see what the result of this wordless interchange would be.

Darcy spoke first. "Miss Starbuck, I don't suppose you'd have any way of knowing that Tom Buck was helping me with a series of stories I'm planning for our newspaper."

"No. That's not the sort of information Tom would have reported. What are your stories about?"

"Well..." Darcy hesitated for a moment, then went on, "They started out as general stories about how important lumber is to this part of Oregon."

"That's hardly a world-shaking subject," Jessie said dryly.

"No. It's the kind of thing we use to fill space when there's no news of real importance," Stone agreed.

"I can understand why Tom would have helped you with the material you'd need," Jessie said. "He was a very kind and helpful man. Not only that, but Tom was one of the first men my father hired when he began branching out into something besides Oriental imports. That's one reason I'm here, of course, it's out of respect to Alex's memory as well as my own interests. But I still don't see—"

Stone interrupted her. "Excuse me, Miss Starbuck, but just a moment ago you said you have confidential information that you'd use in deciding what to do about your Baytown mill."

"Yes, of course I do. Financial reports, details of the mill's operations, information about our customers, especially the large ones we've been losing."

"Suppose," Stone said, "we offered you some confidential information we have? Would you consider that a fair exchange?"

Jessie thought for a moment and then shook her head. "I don't think so. And I can't imagine what sort of confidential information you might have that would interest me, unless it's something Tom Buck told you about the Starbuck mill before he died."

"Our information isn't about your mill," Darcy said.

For the first time, Jessie's interest signaled her that she might be on the verge of getting close to the tie-in that she'd suspected existed, the thread that would connect the fire at the mill and Tom Buck's death with the cartel.

"I could always change my mind, of course," Jessie said slowly. "But I'd want to be sure that any information I might give you about the Starbuck mill wouldn't be used in your newspaper without my permission."

"If father and I agree not to print your information in the paper or tell it to anyone else, will you share it with us?" Darcy persisted.

"Will you promise that, Miss Stone?" Jessie asked.

"Of course," Darcy answered promptly.

"Newspaper people know how to keep confidences, Miss Starbuck," Stone added. "If we say we won't print something or talk about it, you can trust us not to."

Jessie made her decision. "Very well. I'll tell you. The reason I'm uncertain whether to rebuild the Baytown mill or let it stay closed is that it's operated at a loss for the past two years."

After a moment of thoughtful silence, Eli Stone said, "I can't understand that. Tom Buck and I were close friends, but he never mentioned to me that the mill was losing money."

"Of course he didn't!" Jessie said. "That's information he wouldn't have given anyone except me."

"It ties in!" Darcy exclaimed suddenly. "It ties Dodds and his mill into the picture! What he's been doing there was worrying Tom, that's why he was ready to help me. He couldn't understand what Dodds was giving customers to make them stop buying from the Starbuck mill."

She looked at her father for confirmation, and he nodded slowly. "Yes, I suppose so, Darcy. Dodds can use his coolies to undercut any lumber mill that pays fair wages."

"Coolies?" Jessie asked. "Chinese coolies?"

"Sure," Stone replied. "I didn't know there was any other kind."

"How long had Tom Buck known about this?" Jessie frowned.

"Not until a few days before the fire," Stone replied. "But nobody else knew what Dodds was doing either, until Darcy uncovered it."

"That would explain a lot of things," Jessie said, as much to herself as to the others. "Tom wouldn't have had time to get word to me about what the other mill was doing. And it might explain the fire too, and why Tom died in it." She looked at Darcy. "How long has this been going on, Miss Stone?"

"I don't know," Darcy answered. "And—could I ask you a favor before we go any further, Miss Starbuck? Could you just call me Darcy, instead of Miss Stone?"

Jessie smiled. "I'll be glad to, if you'll forget Starbuck and call me Jessie. I answer to it a lot better."

"Does that take me in, too?" Stone asked. "My first name's Eli, in case you've forgotten."

"Of course it does," Jessie said. "Now, since I've told you my confidential news, suppose you tell me yours. The only person I'll share it with is Ki, and I'll promise you that he won't say a word until the time is right."

"As far as I can tell," Darcy began, "Dodds has been using coolie labor for two years, and I suspect it really started almost three years ago."

"But it's not against the law in Oregon to hire coolies, is it? I know that California passed a law a couple of years ago to keep any more Chinese from coming into the state, but that didn't stop anyone from hiring those who were already here."

"Neither did the same kind of law that Oregon passed, and Washington as well," Darcy agreed. "But the laws in all three states do make it illegal for anyone to import a shipload of Chinese to be used as laborers, the way the Southern Pacific Railroad did some years ago."

"And that's what you think Dodds is doing?" Jessie asked. Her quick mind had already told her that this was exactly the kind of thing the cartel would do to injure a business its members wanted to absorb, to drive to bankruptcy.

"That's exactly what Darcy has been trying to find out," Eli Stone said.

"But bringing in a shipload of men, that's a big job! How could they get away with it?" Jessie caught the slip of her tongue too late, but decided not to try to correct it. To have done that would have made the Stones suspicious, and it was not part of her plan at this point to bring the cartel into their conversation.

"It wouldn't have been hard," Darcy said. "Fogarty Bay's a very isolated spot, Jessie, or don't you remember it that well?"

"To tell you the truth, I remember very little about it, except that it's a pretty place."

41

"Well, just to refresh your memory," Darcy went on, "the bay is long and narrow, and runs north and south. Your mill is at the south end, between the mouth of the Siletz River and Fogarty Creek. There's a levee across the mouth of the creek, so the creek keeps the millpond full even in the summer."

Jessie nodded. "I remember the creek and the millpond. It fascinated me to watch the men walking over those floating logs, separating them and pulling them up to the hoist that took them to the saws. And it seems to me that Baytown is on the inland side of the creek from the mill."

"That's right," Stone said. "Now, Fogarty Bay's almost eight miles long, Jessie, and Dodds's Mill is at the north end of the bay. Glenden's the closest town, and it's about six miles from the mill. It couldn't be any closer because there's a stretch of tidal flats just inland from the bay."

"I can see how smuggling in even a shipload of Chinese would be fairly easy, under those circumstances," Jessie said.

"Dodds made it even easier," Darcy told her. "About three years ago he put a ten-foot fence around the mill, and started keeping visitors out. Then he closed the mill for two months, and when he reopened it, there was a lot of talk in Glenden because he didn't hire back any of the men who'd worked there before."

"Surely somebody was curious enough to visit the mill and find out why!" Jessie exclaimed.

"Oh, a lot of poeple were curious, and some of them did try to find out what was going on. But nobody ever did, or if they found out, they didn't come back to tell about it. You see, the mill office is inside the ten-foot fence, and it's closed off from the rest of the mill by an eight-foot fence. Nobody got past that second fence when they went out to see Dodds."

"You seem to have found out a great deal about the

Dodds mill, Darcy," Jessie frowned. "Why?"

"I guess almost everybody would call it a woman's curiosity," Darcy smiled. Then her face grew serious and she added, "I'm really a pretty good reporter, Jessie. When I smell a mystery, I can't seem to stop until I've gotten to the bottom of it."

"Do you feel that you've gotten to the bottom of the Dodds mystery?"

Eli answered instead of Darcy. "No, Jessie. There are a lot of things that we're still curious about. But Darcy hasn't stopped working on it yet. In fact—" He stopped short.

"Now you've got my curiosity aroused," Jessie said. "Go on, Eli. In fact, what?"

"I think Father was about to say that there are still some loose ends to the story that I'm trying to tie up now, before we print anything," Darcy said.

"I've got a feeling there's more to it than that," Jessie told her. "Now I've told you what you wanted to know, Darcy. I expect you to treat me just as openly."

For a moment, Darcy did not reply. Then she said, "It's not that I don't want to tell you everything, Jessie. I don't know myself what the loose ends are."

"Darcy was all ready to start writing her story," Eli put in. "Then Tom told her that she'd better wait a few days because he had a hint that something was going to happen that would make it a bigger story than ever."

"And he didn't go any further?" Jessie asked.

Darcy shook her head. "All he'd say was that it was important. I don't really know where he was getting his information, or what he was expecting to learn. The last time I talked to him was the day before the fire. He told me that he ought to have the information within the next few days."

"Then, when Tom died in the fire, he still hadn't given

you any hint as to what the information was?"

"No. But I'll share it with you as soon as I dig it up, Jessie, if you're still in Baytown."

"I'm going to Baytown to get the real facts about the fire at the mill and Tom Buck's death," Jessie said quickly. "And I intend to stay there until I'm positive I have them."

"Since Tom died, I've been doing some investigating of my own," Darcy told her. "He didn't give me much to go on, but I think I've found where he was getting his information about Dodds, and—"

Darcy did not finish what she'd started to say. Webb's shout from the driver's seat drew the attention of those inside the coach away from their conversation.

"We've come to Rickreall," Eli said as the coach began to slow down. "And it's starting to drizzle. But once we get rid of those outlaws' bodies and turn the live one over to the town marshal, we ought to make better time unless this rain gets heavy enough to soak the road. But we'll still be late getting into Baytown."

Webb pulled up the stage in front of the town marshal's office, and he and Stone went inside, taking the surviving holdup man with them, to persuade the marshal to take responsibility for attending to the burial of the dead men and delivering the survivor to the county authorities at Salem. While they were talking to the marshal, Jessie and Ki stepped under the canopy that sheltered the plank sidewalk in front of the office long enough to exchange a few quick words.

Ki told her, "I got the holdup man to talk to me. They were just cowhands down on their luck, trying to get a few dollars from anybody who came along, not killers after us. But I didn't have any way of knowing that, Jessie. I had to do what I did."

Jessie nodded. "You saved somebody else from being held up, perhaps shot. But I've been having an interesting talk with Eli Stone and his daughter. There isn't time to tell

44

you all of it now, but I'm more positive than ever that my hunch about the cartel being involved in burning the mill was a good one."

Jessie stopped as the door of the marshal's office opened. Eli Stone, hobbling on his crutch, came out, followed by Darcy. They started toward Jessie and Ki. Beyond them, Jessie saw the marshal leading the three horses away. The bodies of the two dead bandits still lay across the back of one of the animals, and the third man, she supposed, had been locked up. Webb had come out of the marshal's office now, and was standing by the stagecoach, waiting to start again. The mist that had been drizzling down had become a light rain, and Webb was pulling on a slicker.

Leaning on his crutch, Stone said, "We're just about ready to start." He turned to Ki. "I hope you'll change your mind about riding with us inside the coach. We can put that big crate of Darcy's in the boot to make room for you."

"What about your leg?" Ki asked.

"That won't be any problem," Darcy told him. "You sit next to Father, where I've been sitting, I'll sit by Jessie, where the box was, and father can put his foot up by me."

"I've already apologized for the fool mistake I made," Eli said. "And it looks like we're all going to be working together to find out..." He shook his head and said, "It's too long a story to tell you now. But I hope you'll change your mind and ride with us inside."

Jessie said, "It would be a good idea, Ki. It's really starting to rain now, and there's no reason for you to get soaked."

Ki nodded. "You're right. Let's get the box in the boot, then. Webb looks like he's getting impatient to start."

They made the necessary changes quickly, and in a few minutes the stagecoach resumed its interrupted journey, under a gray sky from which the rain continued to fall with increasing force.

45

★

Chapter 5

"Well, there it is," Eli said, pointing across the broad alluvial valley to an almost invisible huddle of houses that, in the clear morning light, could just be seen in the distance. "Baytown. Not as far away as it looks, either. Another four hours and we'll be sitting down to breakfast."

Webb had stopped the stage to rest the horses after the long pull up the final ridge of the Coast Range foothills. Jessie, Ki, Darcy, and Eli had gotten out to stretch, glad of a chance to escape briefly from the swaying and jouncing that had kept them from sleeping more than a few minutes at a time during the long, rainy night.

Though there'd been frequent stops during the hours of luminous darkness, the rain had kept the passengers from getting any real ease during the short periods when they'd left the cramped confinement of the narrow coach. They'd hurried to the bushes to relieve themselves and returned to the shelter of the coach as quickly as possible.

With daybreak the rain had stopped, and now the crystal air was filled with the dancing twinkles of the early sun caught by the raindrops that clung to the towering firs. The huge trees marched up from the wide, shallow Siletz valley, along the flanks of the rising ground. Along the rim of the valley, the Coast Range was more hills than mountains, though to the north there were higher green-clad peaks. In

46

the Siletz valley, the high trees stopped halfway down the flanks of the ridges, but to the north, where the ridges and humped peaks extended to the ocean, the trees grew to the water's edge.

To the south, other rugged hills were visible beyond the valley through which the greenish waters of the Siletz River zigzagged in sinuous curves and sweeps that would have been the envy of a snake. The river flowed in a general northwesterly course, and from the ridge could be seen the thin, shining strip of Fogarty Bay. Across a spit of land which, from the distance, looked to be only finger-wide, the Pacific Ocean stretched in its immensity, an endless expanse of tossing, pointed whitecaps from the shoreline to the horizon.

In the eyes of the quartet viewing it from the ridge, Baytown was a series of sketchy vertical and horizontal lines. No details of its buildings were visible from such a distance, and its houses showed only as a geometrically precise anomaly, the single manmade patch in a landscape of rounded rises and curved ridges that marked the courses of tiny creeks and rills.

"You can see where your mill stood, Jessie," Eli said when he noticed her eyes fixed on the bay. "It was just beyond the town, right by the mouth of the river. That's why it did so well. The current from the river and the creek kept the silt from piling up there, so even in summer, when the river was low, ships didn't have to wait for a high tide to come in and load up."

Jessie nodded absently, without taking her eyes from the valley. "And Dodds's mill—it's at the other end of the bay?"

"Yes," Darcy volunteered. "But you can't see it from here, it's behind that little hump." She pointed, then moved her finger to indicate a point still farther inland. "And Glenden's in back of that line of trees that you see east of the upper end of the bay."

Ki had said nothing. He stood a little apart from the others, his eyes fixed on the horizon. Jessie recognized his mood; she'd seen it often during their Hawaiian stay. She knew that Ki's mind was on his homeland, the country in which his mixed parentage had made him an outcast, the country which, in his pain and grief, he'd renounced to migrate to America.

"If you folks got the kinks outta your legs, we better roll," Webb announced. "We still got a ways to go, and it won't get no shorter whilst we stand around gawking."

During the rest of the journey, there was little conversation in the coach. After they'd left Rickreall, Ki had been told of the discussions between Jessie and the Stones that had taken place while he was riding with the prisoner, but after that there had been little left to say. The jolting and swaying of the stage through a long, sleepless night had tired all of them, and when at last the coach creaked to a stop in front of the hotel in Baytown, food and a bed were all that any of them could think of.

"I know you'll want to take a look at what's left of your mill," Eli told Jessie as they said their goodbyes in front of the hotel. "And Darcy and I have to see to the paper."

"I keep telling father not to worry," Darcy said. "I got this week's edition of the *Gazette* almost ready to go to press before I left for Salem, so we won't have too much to do."

"I'm going to sleep before I do anything," Jessie said.

"By the day after tomorrow, I should have that last bit of information that Tom Buck was trying to get," Darcy told her. "How would you and Ki like to have dinner with us then? You'll have news for us, I'm sure, and with any luck, we should have some for you."

"And if you need anything in the meantime, the *Gazette* office is just around the corner from the hotel," Eli added.

In the late afternoon, refreshed by sleep and a bountiful meal of baked deviled Dungeness crab, Jessie and Ki walked to the edge of Baytown, where the business office of the burned-out mill was located in its own small frame building.

A short distance beyond the office, Fogarty Creek flowed sluggishly. A bridge spanned the creek, with a well-beaten path leading to it. There was a broad spit of land between the creek and the mouth of the Siletz River, and as Jessie and Ki drew close to the office, they could see that the spit was covered with ashes, their gray surface broken here and there by the cast-iron frameworks of saws and planing tables.

They stopped for a few moments to look at the devastated area, then Jessie shrugged and led the way into the office. The stooped, white-bearded bookkeeper, sitting at his desk inside, blinked with surprise and then broke into a smile when he saw Jessie enter.

"Miss Starbuck!" he exclaimed. "I've been hoping since the fire that you'd find time to come out here, but all I've had is a letter from your man at the ranch saying he'd sent word to you."

"He did, and I started just as soon as I got the news, Mr. Sawtell," Jessie replied, shaking the bookkeeper's slim pale hand.

"It's good to see you again, after such a long time," Sawtell went on. "But I know how busy you must've been."

Jessie nodded and said, "You remember Ki, I'm sure. He was with my father on the last visit he made to Baytown. Now Ki is helping me."

"Of course I remember you," Sawtell told Ki. "But when you were here with Mr. Starbuck, you didn't stay long

49

enough for us really to get acquainted." He turned back to Jessie. "I hate to welcome you back at such a sad time, Miss Starbuck. Tom was a fine man, and I know you'll miss him, just like we do."

"Of course I will. But since you were here when the mill burned, you know a great deal more than I do about what happened, and the first thing I'd like to do is sit down and have you tell Ki and me exactly what happened."

For the next quarter hour, interrupting him now and then to ask a question, Jessie and Ki listened to the bookkeeper as he recounted the events of the night when the mill was destroyed.

Sawtell had been at home in Baytown when the flames shot through the roof of the main mill structure shortly before midnight. By the time he'd reached the mill, the entire central section and the working bays were engulfed in flames. The millworkers, all of whom lived in town, had already formed bucket brigades from the mouth of the river, but the intense heat kept them from getting close enough to the building for the water to have any effect on the fiercely blazing walls. In the end, all the men could do was to stand clear and watch as the great timber beams that supported the roof burned through and collapsed.

"After that, we just had to wait till the ashes cooled down enough for us to get up to what was left," he said. "And that wasn't for two days. I was certain Tom was dead, when he didn't show up while the fire was burning. I knew he'd have been there unless something had happened to him, and all I could think of was that he'd been working in his office when the fire broke out and didn't notice anything wrong until it was too late for him to get outside. I thought maybe he'd dozed off, something like that."

"And you found his body in the office?" Jessie asked.

"No. That's puzzled me, Miss Starbuck, just like how the fire got started has been on my mind a lot. There wasn't much left of Tom to find, by the time the fire burned out, but what we did find of his body was up near the front, close to the loading dock. There was an outside door just around the corner from his office. If he'd gone out of it, he'd have gotten away."

"You're positive it was Tom Buck's body that you found?" Ki asked.

"Oh, yes, Mr. Ki. There was what was left of his gold watch, enough to be sure it was his. And his pocketknife too, with part of the ivory handle still on it. That was Tom's body, all right."

"I don't suppose there was any way of telling where the fire started, or how?" Jessie asked.

Sawtell shook his head. "No way that I could tell. Of course, there never was any kind of fire allowed in the mill, not even cigars or pipes and matches. That fine sawdust that gathers around the saws and shapers—once it gets dry, it goes up almost like gunpowder, you know."

"How about the engines that ran all the machinery?" Ki asked. "It seems to me that I remember them being away from the main building, with the drive belts running through a covered raceway."

Sawtell nodded. "All the donkeys that furnished power for the saws and planers were twenty feet from the main building, just to make sure they wouldn't start a fire."

"We'd better go out and see for ourselves what things look like, Ki," Jessie said. "I'm sure there's nothing but ashes to look at, but I want to see the place, just the same."

"Do you want me to wait here until you come back, Miss Jessie?" the bookkeeper asked. "I'd be glad to."

Jessie shook her head. "You go home if we're not back by the time you usually leave. Anything that Ki or I might have to ask you about can wait until tomorrow."

As they left the office and started across the bridge to the layer of ashes covering the ground where the mill had stood, Ki said, "I don't expect to find anything worth looking at, Jessie. From here it looks as though the fire didn't leave anything for us to find."

"I know, Ki. But I suppose I've just got to look to satisfy myself that nobody's overlooked something that might give us a clue to what happened."

They stopped at the margin of the burned-out area and stood looking at what had been a busy lumber mill. At close range it was possible to tell where each piece of machinery had stood, for the cast-iron frames of the saws and planers rose above the three-inch-deep layer of gray ashes. Where there had been columns and trusses that supported the roof, the sturdy iron braces that had reinforced the joints were piled in untidy heaps of scrap, already beginning to show signs of rust.

To the left of where Jessie and Ki were standing, small metal shacks, the sides that were facing the mill warped and twisted from the intense heat, housed the donkey engines that had provided power for the machinery. In front of most of them, the charred ends of the broad, thick leather belts that had run between the donkeys and the machines lay in stiff, untidy curls.

Jessie pointed to what was left of an iron doorframe. "That's where the door was. Tom's office was just beyond it. I can't imagine why he didn't get out, no matter how bad the fire was."

"Sawtell told us they found his body near the loading dock," Ki said thoughtfully. He looked across the ashes to the river, where the charred tops of wooden pilings protruded above the surface of the water. "That would be the dock, over there." Measuring the distance with his eyes, he shook his head. "Jessie, that's almost two hundred yards."

After she'd looked across the space to which Ki pointed, Jessie said, "Yes. But what difference does that make? Tom must have been running across to dive into the river or something like that. His clothing might have been on fire."

Ki shook his head. "No. If the fire was as intense as both Sawtell and the Stones say it was, the man hasn't been born who could run that far. The heat would sear his lungs to a cinder, and he'd drop before he'd gone more than fifty or sixty feet."

"Then maybe Tom ran toward the dock before the fire got so intense," Jessie suggested.

"If it had happened that way, he'd have been able to reach the dock and dive into the river," Ki frowned.

"What difference does it make, Ki?" Jessie asked, an edge of irritation in her tone. "The main thing is that Tom didn't get out alive."

"It could make a lot of difference," Ki replied. "I didn't know Tom Buck well; I think I talked with him only two or three times, when I was here with Alex. But he didn't impress me as a man who'd be easy to panic."

"No," Jessie agreed. "Tom had a very cool head. But I still don't see what point you're trying to make."

"Think about it a minute, Jessie. If the fire was getting close to its peak, Tom Buck wouldn't have tried to reach the loading dock. He wouldn't have started through the flames if he'd seen that they were too high for him to make it. In that case, he'd have gone out the door close to his office. If the fire hadn't reached its peak, he was close enough to the dock to have gotten away. All he had to do was cover the fifteen or twenty feet between him and the dock and jump into the river."

Jessie studied the ash-heaped area for a few moments, then slowly nodded. "It took long enough to sink in, but I see now what you're getting at. Tom had almost gotten to the dock, which he couldn't have reached from his office if the fire had peaked. He didn't get to the dock because something stopped him twenty feet away."

"Exactly," Ki said soberly. "The question is, who or what stopped him where his body was found."

"I don't suppose we'll ever know the answer. Tom's the only one who knew why he stopped."

"I'm going to look for an answer, though. You stay here if you don't want to get your shoes full of ashes. I'm going to slip mine off and go over there to look."

"How'll you know where to look?" Jessie objected.

"There'll be footprints in the ashes, I can backtrack on them. They'll lead me to the spot where Tom's body was found. You wait here."

"I will not wait here!" Jessie snapped. She began slipping off her shoes. "I'm going with you!"

Wading through ashes that were sometimes heaped almost knee-high, they started across the burned-out area, walking to one side of the tracks that Ki was certain had been left by the party carrying Tom Buck's remains out of the debris. Less than twenty feet from the char-topped pilings that marked the spot where the loading dock had been, Ki halted at a place where the footprints merged and overlapped in confusion around a small clear space on the packed-earth floor.

"This is the spot," he said positively. "There were five men who came here and went back carrying something. You can see the tracks clearly enough; they're scattered heading this way and close together in an orderly pattern when they were heading back, carrying what remained of Tom's body to where the mill door was."

"What do you expect to find?" Jessie asked.

"I don't know. I'm just hoping I'll find something."

Ki hunkered down beside the cleared spot and began exploring the thin coating of light ash that had settled on it. He combed his fingertips through it methodically, working in one direction until he'd covered the entire spot, then he changed his position to go over the same area, this time drawing his fingers across it at right angles to the lines left by his first search. He'd made only a half-dozen passes when his hand stopped and he began very carefully dusting off the thin coating of drifted ash to expose in the dark earth a spot about two inches in diameter.

Jessie saw light reflected from the brown soil and asked, "What have you found, Ki?"

He did not reply for a moment. His head was bent close to the floor and his fingers were busy around the spot where Jessie had seen the reflection. Looking up, he extended his hand for her to get a close look at the dark mottled blob of shiny material he'd unearthed.

"What is it?" she asked.

"Glass. Glass that's been melted and fused by heat into a different shape from the one it was in orginally. You remember that Sawtell said they'd found Tom's watch? My guess is that this is the crystal."

"How can you be sure?"

"I can't. But as close as this spot is to the dock, I don't think anything made of glass would be lying on the surface unless it had just fallen there. In a day or two of work, the loaders would've ground it into the dirt."

"Does it prove anything, though, Ki?"

"Nothing except that we're in the right spot. And if Tom Buck was like most of the men around here, he carried his watch in his lower vest pocket or in the fob pocket of his pants."

Carefully keeping his feet away from the bare spot, Ki bent over and with his forefinger drew the rough outline of a man's body in the ashes. The waist of the outline was centered on the place where he'd discovered the bit of fused glass.

"That's just about the place where the watch would have been if it had been in either his trousers or vest pocket," he explained when he saw Jessie's frown of curiosity. "Now

I'll clear the area inside the outline and go over it just as I did the small section I searched first."

While Jessie watched, Ki began his methodical search. He criss-crossed the space representing the torso, then took off his headband and began dusting away the residue of fine ash left covering the soil within the outlined shoulders and chest. He'd worked halfway down the space when he stopped with a sharp exclamation of satisfaction. Straightening up, he pointed to a small gray cylinder lying on the dirt.

Jessie bent over and peered at the object. "It looks like— Ki, it is a bullet, isn't it?"

"Yes. The bullet that killed Tom Buck, probably when he was chasing whoever set the mill on fire."

"Why didn't it melt, though?"

"It didn't melt because it was inside Tom's body until the fire cooled down."

"But how did you know it was there?"

"I didn't, Jessie. All I knew was that there had to be an explanation for Tom's body being found here. The only one I could think of was that he had a reason for coming to this spot, and that he got here before the fire had spread over the entire building. That had to mean he was chasing whoever touched off the fire. Oh, of course, I suspected that Tom had been shot by whoever he was chasing, but I had to find proof."

"And that's exactly what you did!" Jessie exclaimed.

Ki bent down and picked up the bullet. He looked at it closely and said, "It's a .41. Not the most common caliber for a pistol anymore."

Jessie had been lost in thought. She said suddenly, "Ki, do you suppose it was somebody Tom recognized who shot him?"

"It wouldn't surprise me. Either that, or whoever shot him knew he could be identified and probably connected

56

with whoever ordered the fire set. And I'm sure you're thinking the same thing I am, Jessie."

"I'm sure I am too. Someone who could be traced back to Dodds's mill. Ki, I think it's time we really went to work. We'll go and have a look at the Dodds outfit tomorrow!"

★

Chapter 6

"Horses, Miss Starbuck?" The clerk behind the desk of the hotel raised his eyebrows in surprise, as though he found the very idea of renting a saddle horse either amusing or preposterous or both. "I'm afraid the livery stable here doesn't have any saddle horses to rent."

"How do people who don't own a horse travel from one place to another, then?" Jessie asked.

"By boat, of course. Unless they want to go inland; in which case they ride the stage."

"I see. When does the next stage leave for Glenden?"

"Let's see, this is Thursday. The next stage will be going on Monday."

Jessie held back the sharp retort that was at the tip of her tongue. Her blue eyes snapping and darkening with anger, she asked, "Supposing I must get there today?"

"In that case, Miss Starbuck, you should go down to the dock and find Amos Weatherby. Amos has some very good skiffs and dinghies, and his rental rates are quite moderate."

"Thank you," Jessie said, controlling her impulse to say something entirely different. She turned away from the desk just as Ki came downstairs. Going across the lobby, Jessie reached the foot of the stairs at the same time that he did.

"Ki!" she exclaimed indignantly. "Do you know there

aren't any saddle horses to rent in this town? The hotel clerk says people here travel by boat!"

"Since Baytown's on the seacoast, I don't suppose that's too unusual," Ki replied calmly. "In a place like this, it's usually easier to get from one place to another by boat than on horseback."

"But I've never sailed a boat in my life!"

"I have, Jessie, many times. I suppose we can rent a small boat at one of the docks that must be along the bay-front?"

"Yes. A man named Amos Weatherby has boats for rent."

"Then we will have breakfast, and after we've eaten, we'll go and rent one of Mr. Weatherby's boats and sail up the bay to Dodds's mill."

Over the breakfast table, Jessie asked, "Are you sure you can sail a boat, Ki?"

"I learned to handle a boat before I was large enough to sit in the saddle of a horse. Remember, Jessie, Japan is a land of many islands, where boats and the sea are very important."

"I hadn't thought of it that way. But I'd still feel better if we were going on horseback."

"We'll get there faster and more comfortably."

"Before we leave, Ki, I want to go up to my room and get my pistol out of my luggage. Are you going to wear yours?"

Ki shook his head and tapped his right forearm, where the sheath containing his *shuriken* was concealed under the loose sleeve of his blouse. Then he leaned back in his chair and showed Jessie the butt of the short double-edged knife he carried in the waistband of his trousers. "If there's trouble," he said, "I'd rather not be carrying any obvious weapons."

59

"Yes. Let's don't seem to be looking for trouble, not this time, at least. I'll carry the Colt in my handbag."

At the boat dock after breakfast, they found Amos Weatherby to be the picture of a salt-caked sailor, from the grizzled fringe of beard wreathing his tanned face to the pegleg that replaced his own left leg below the knee. He offered them the choice of three small boats, and Ki quickly decided on a fourteen-foot skiff with a balance lugsail, explaining to Jessie that the sail was akin to the lateen sail of the small Japanese craft with which he was familiar. He was sure it would not present any problems to him.

Nor did it. After a few minor yaws before he'd gotten the feel of the tiller, Ki set the sail to take advantage of the wind blowing steadily and briskly in from the ocean, and the skiff bore smartly north in the center of the narrow bay.

Jessie had not sailed before in a small boat. She was surprised to discover that her perspective on her surroundings was entirely different from that to which she'd grown accustomed.

On the back of a horse, looking down from even that small height seemed to reduce distances; sitting in the skiff's prow, her eyes less than a yard above the water, looking up at the land made the distance to shore seem very great. Though she knew that Fogarty Bay was small, only five or six miles across, the shore on both sides seemed far away, and the north end of the bay toward which they were sailing appeared to be an infinite distance they would never span.

"How long is it going to take us to get there?" she asked.

"Not very long."

"We don't seem to be moving very fast."

"Faster than you think. Don't look at the shore on either side, Jessie. Look ahead and watch how that fence around Dodds's mill grows higher as we get closer to it."

To Jessie's surprise, the high fence that surrounded the mill on the sharply curving north shore of the bay appeared to grow wider and higher in a very short time. Jessie had not yet become accustomed to looking up, or to judging distances across a smooth unbroken expanse of water that offered no landmarks by which the skiff's forward progress could be gauged.

Suddenly the fence that enclosed the mill was only a few hundred yards in front of them, and she could see the roof of the main building above it, and the plumes of thin smoke that rose from the donkey engines powering the machinery. Details of the shoreline came into focus: a loading dock on the side of the fence nearest the ocean; a slough in which the cylindrical shapes of brown- and tan-barked logs broke the water's surface.

As they drew closer to shore, she could hear the nasal whine of saws and the higher-pitched shrilling of the planers that smoothed the edges and surfaces of the rough-cut boards after they'd come from the saw carriage. The smell of warmed resin mingled with the salt-tangy air.

A small pier extended from the shore near the center of the fence, which was set back from the shoreline. Ki dropped the sail and their forward motion slowed perceptibly. He picked up the oar that lay along the thwarts and fended the boat off the pier, letting it swing close enough for him to step up to the wooden walkway and moor the little vessel. He pulled the skiff and held it against the pier while Jessie stepped ashore and they started up the path to the gate in the ten-foot fence that rose a few yards from shore.

They reached the gate and Ki pushed it experimentally. It did not yield an inch. He clenched his hand into a fist and pounded on the rough-grained wood. A few moments passed before feet grated on the other side of the gate. Bars slid back with a squeak and a final thud, and the gate opened a few inches. Part of a man's face appeared, framed into a slit by the edges of the gate so that all Ki and Jessie could see were his eyes, nose, and mouth. The eyes were slitted in suspicion, the corners of the mouth turned down in a scowl. To their surprise, the man inside the gate seemed to be expecting them.

"Oh," he said to Ki. "You'd be the Chinaman the boss has been looking for." Before Ki could correct him, the man went on, "Come on in." He started to swing the gate open, then hesitated and said, "He didn't say nothing about a woman, but I guess if she's with you, it's all right."

He swung the gate open wide enough to allow Ki and Jessie to enter. They exchanged quick glances, but hesitated only momentarily before going through the opening. While the man closed and barred the heavy gate, Ki and Jessie looked around curiously. The arrangement fitted the description Darcy Stone had given Jessie while they were talking on the stagecoach.

They were in a small square enclosure, formed by an inner fence lower than the one that stood behind them and circled the mill. Over the top of the inner fence they could see the eaves of the main mill building and as far down the wall as the tops of its windows. Within the inner enclosure there was only one building, a small square frame structure butted against the inside fence, next to a second gate. It too was closed.

Pointing to the building, the gate guard said, "Come along. The boss has been waiting for you to get here."

Ki started to speak, but Jessie stopped him by shaking her head. They followed their guide to the building and went inside. The room they entered was narrow and bare. Two doors broke the wall that divided it from the remainder of the building, and both of them were closed. The guard knocked at one of the doors.

Jessie and Ki took stock of their surroundings while they waited. A wide window cut into the back wall of the room opened the mill yard to their view. Jessie almost gasped as

62

she looked out, but caught herself in time to cut off the involuntary exclamation that was rising to her lips. There were only a few men moving about between the inner fence and the wall of the mill, but they were all Chinese. A few of them were bare to the waist, but most of them wore the blue cotton work-blouses that were the mark of the coolie class.

She and Ki had only a few moments to look out the rear window before the door on which their guide had knocked swung open. A stocky man wearing a dark suit, a derby hat pushed back on his head, stood in the opening. He had a cigar clenched between his teeth, and his blubbery lips worked unpleasantly as he looked at them with washed-out blue eyes and asked their guide, "What in hell you want, Gooch?"

"This is the Chinaman you been looking for, Mr. Dodds. The gal was with him, so I figured it was all right to let both of 'em come on in."

Dodds nodded and dismissed the man with a wave. He took a step toward Ki and said, "You'd be Quong Sun, I guess?"

"Your guess would be incorrect, Mr. Dodds," Ki said pleasantly. "My name is Ki."

"Ki what?" Dodds frowned.

"Just Ki."

"Quong Sun didn't say he'd send somebody else, dammit! He told me he'd come hisself!" Dodds growled. He looked at Jessie and added, "And he didn't say nothing about a woman being mixed up in our deal."

"Your friend Quong Sun did not send me," Ki said smoothly. He watched Dodds closely as he added, "Allow me, Mr. Dodds, to introduce you to Miss Jessica Starbuck."

"Starbuck!" Dodds exploded. He turned to Jessie and asked angrily, "How the hell did you get in here?"

All the lessons on strategy and tactics that Jessie had

been given by Alex Starbuck came to her aid. She said calmly, "The usual way, Mr. Dodds. Through a door that one of your men opened for me without any request on my part. And as long as I'm here, I suggest that we talk sensibly, not angrily."

"I don't like to do business with women," Dodds said. "You belong at home, not here. You look like you ain't old enough yet to be dry behind your ears."

"But I am here, Mr. Dodds. And I'll take your remark about my age as a compliment instead of an insult. Now, would you like to invite me into your office, where we can sit down and talk?"

"What about the chink?" Dodds asked. "Who is he and what's he doing with you?"

"Ki works with me, just as he did with my father. He is also my friend. He is not Chinese. I'm sure he has as much American blood in his veins as you do."

Dodds puffed his cigar, filling the doorway with smoke. He looked from Jessie to Ki before saying, "I'll talk to you, Miss Starbuck. By ourselves and in private. Take it or leave it."

Jessie told Ki, "Since this is Mr. Dodds's office, I suppose it's his privilege to say that. Very well, Mr. Dodds." To Ki she added, "What we have to talk about shouldn't take long, Ki."

"Of course," Ki nodded. "I'll wait here."

Jessie swept through the doorway into Dodds's office, brushing past the guard as though he did not exist. Without waiting for an invitation, she sat down in the chair that stood in front of his paper-littered desk, and waited for him to sit down.

While she waited, Jessie glanced quickly around the office. Like the anteroom, it had a window in the back wall giving a view of the mill. A door next to the window opened directly into the yard. A rope, its end knotted to form a handle, passed through the wall next to the window and hung halfway to the floor. Some sort of signal bell, Jessie thought, must be on the other end. The walls of the office were bare except for a large calendar on which two days of the current month were circled in red crayon. Jessie abandoned her inspection as Dodds closed the door to the anteroom and started for his desk.

Dodds was obviously uncomfortable. He settled into the chair behind the desk and paid no attention to Jessie while he busied himself for a moment shoving first to one side and the other the scattered, piled-up papers that covered the desktop. Jessie realized quite well that he was hoping to force her to speak first. She looked past him at the wall calendar. Finally, Dodds could not hold back his curiosity any longer.

"Well?" he said. "You came here to see me, Miss Starbuck. Get down to business, if you've got something to talk about."

"I don't think we need to go through any preliminaries," Jessie said quietly. "You know very well that my mill was burned, and I strongly suspect you know a great deal more than I do about that fire."

"Now, wait a minute!" Dodds broke in. "If you're hinting that I had anything to do with that fire, you're wrong!"

"Mr. Dodds," Jessie replied, "there's no need for you to deny anything, unless you feel guilty."

"Well, dammit, you just as good as said—"

Jessie was pleased at having drawn first blood. She told Dodds, "Perhaps you misunderstood me. You were here when the fire occurred. I was several thousand miles away."

"Oh. Maybe I did take your meaning wrong, at that. Well, go on. You sure didn't come here to tell me something I already know."

"Of course not." Quite casually she went on, "I came here to offer to buy your mill."

For a moment, Dodds stared incredulously at Jessie, then he asked her, "What gave you the idea my mill's for sale?"

"That should be obvious. No one likes to lose money, Mr. Dodds, and you must be losing a great deal by cutting the price of lumber the way you have been for the past year or more."

A note of triumph in his voice, Dodds replied, "And it lost your mill a lot of customers because your prices were so much higher'n mine, didn't it?"

"Yes. We both know that. I'd be a fool to deny it."

"But you got the idea it cost me a lot to undercut you."

"I know the cost of operating a lumber mill. You cannot possibly be making a profit at the prices you're getting. You must be quite short of money after cutting your prices as low as you have."

"Well, it just happens you're wrong. Maybe I learned some things you haven't yet."

"Perhaps you have. One of them seems to be that you can hire Chinese for lower wages than you'd pay American workers. I suppose the ones you have here are all legal immigrants?"

"They are, and I got the papers to prove it."

Jessie was tempted to point out that immigration papers could be forged quite easily. Instead she hurried to cure her mistake in even opening the subject of Dodds's Chinese laborers. She said quickly, "I didn't come to talk about your workmen. It's the mill I'm interested in. We have orders to fill, and it's not a Starbuck habit to default on obligations."

"Now that's just too bad, ain't it?" Dodds smiled. "But I might be—"

A knock at the door that opened into the mill yard interrupted him. Dodds went to the door, opened it, and Jessie got a quick glimpse of a huge shaven-headed Chinese man standing outside. Dodds looked over his shoulder at her, but Jessie had seen his head start to turn and she was now looking down into her handbag.

"I'll be right back," Dodds said over his shoulder.

He went outside, closing the door behind him. Jessie could not resist the opportunity. She craned her neck to get a look at the papers scattered on Dodds's desk, and one of them seemed to leap into sharp relief. It was the top edge of a sheet of letterhead bearing the engraved words FARMERS' & MECHANICS' BANK, the bank that, before his death, Alex had suspected so strongly of being owned by the cartel. The text of the letter was covered, and Jessie made no effort to read it. She settled back into her chair and was glancing out the window when Dodds came back in.

"One of my foremen," Dodds said curtly, and without further explanation or apology he picked up the conversation where they had left off. "I was about to say I might be persuaded to fill your orders, if we can make the right kind of deal."

"I wouldn't be interested in that," Jessie said curtly. "I would be interested in paying you a fair price for your mill. In cash, I might point out."

"Well, I don't doubt you got the cash to throw around," he replied. "But I don't happen to need money, Miss Starbuck. I've got all I can use and more where that came from." He stopped and his eyes narrowed as he studied Jessie's face. When she did not react to his statement, Dodds went on, "I might as well tell you now, instead of waiting for you to find out about it later. I'm planning to enlarge my mill as fast as I can. That'll let me take away what's left of your customers during the year or so it'll take you to get your mill back into operation."

"It's your privilege to try to do that," Jessie said calmly. "Just as it's my privilege to—"

Her words were cut off by a report almost as loud and sharp as a pistol shot. Dodds swiveled to look out the window, and Jessie's eyes followed his.

She saw one of the mill's blue-clad coolie workmen running past, pursued by the giant Chinese who'd talked to Dodds a few moments earlier. The Chinese foreman was wielding a bullwhip. He raised it as Jessie watched and snapped its tip back, then the braided tip sped forward like a snake and wrapped itself around the throat of the running man. The coolie was unable to stop in time to keep the whip from pulling him to the ground. The giant flipped the butt of the weapon to free its coils and lifted it to lash out again.

A crash of glass exploded from the anteroom. Jessie and Dodds both looked around and started for the door. Out of the corner of her eye, Jessie saw Ki land a yard or two from the foreman after his leap through the window. Instead of aiming his whip's cutting blow at the recumbent coolie, the giant switched his aim. The tip swung around. Ki stood directly in its path.

★

Chapter 7

Ki had been standing in the anteroom, looking idly out the window into the mill yard, when the huge Chinese first knocked at the door of Dodds's office. From his size and facial features, Ki had recognized the big man as a Mongolian, a member of the race that had, for centuries, struck terror into the hearts of all other Chinese.

He'd watched while the giant talked to Dodds, and though he could not hear what they were saying, he was able to tell by their gestures and expressions that the Mongolian was complaining and that after hearing his complaint, Dodds had given him an order or instructions of some kind. The Mongolian had gone around the corner of the mill, out of sight, and Ki dismissed the episode from his mind.

A few minutes later, when he'd seen the blue-clad coolie run around the corner of the mill building, followed by the bald giant with a bullwhip, Ki's interest and curiosity had revived. When the whip-wielder caught the coolie by the neck with his lash, dragged him down, and then prepared to whip him while he was still lying on the ground, half-choked, Ki dove through the window. He placed himself where Jessie had seen him, between the giant Mongolian and his victim. He was still standing there, his eyes locked with those of the man with the whip, when Jessie and Dodds burst out of the back door of Dodds's office.

"Ki!" Jessie called. "It's not your fight!"

Without taking his eyes off the giant, Ki shook his head. "I'm making it my fight, Jessie! The coolie hasn't any way to fight back! Somebody's got to help him!"

"Not you, Ki," Jessie said. "We didn't come here for this! I've finished my business with Dodds, it's time for us to go."

"That's good advice," Dodds chimed in. "Da Bao is my foreman. It's his job to keep my men in line, and I won't let you or anybody else tell him what to do!"

"You can punish the coolie some other way," Ki said, still watching Da Bao. "Dock his wages or fire him, but don't let your strawboss beat him to death!"

"Nobody tells me what to do in my own mill, either!" Dodds snapped. "Now do what your boss says and get off my land, or I'll turn Da Bao on you, too!"

"That is your responsibility, Dodds," Ki said coldly. "If you do, you will be to blame for what happens to your foreman."

Dodds turned back to Jessie. "That Chinee's your man, Miss Starbuck. You better get him to listen to you."

Jessie realized that by now the confrontation she'd hoped would not occur had arrived and had gone too far to be reversed. Although in many ways Ki was more American than Oriental, she knew that he retained from his Japanese heritage a keen sense of the opinion held of him by others. It was the intangible quality of an individual's public aspect, which in the Far East is called "face," that would be damaged now if she ordered Ki to back away from the giant Mongolian. Jessie also knew that Ki had defeated far more formidable opponents. She did not reply to Dodds's remark, but merely shook her head.

Dodds was as eager for a confrontation as Jessie was to avoid one. He did not wait after she'd shaken her head, but turned back to the burly foreman and called, "Go on, Da

70

Bao! He's yours! Give him a good lesson!"

The shiny-domed Mongolian needed no further encouragement. He had been standing with his hands at his side, the braided leather bullwhip dangling from his right hand. The whip's tapered nine-foot length stretched like an undulating snake toward Ki, the wicked tassle of its lash extending an arm's length behind him.

When he faced an opponent of such size, one armed with a weapon such as the bullwhip, which in skilled hands could shear off a half-pound of flesh with a slash, or open a cut with the rough braids of its upper length, or burst an eyeball with its tassled tip, it was not Ki's way to rush into an attack. His eyes had already flicked over the foreman's massive body as he sized up Da Bao's capability as an opponent. What he saw would have discouraged an ordinary man.

Da Bao stood four inches taller than Ki. His bald head was massive, melon-shaped, set on a neck so short that there was almost no gap between his protruding chin and his wide shoulders. The giant's biceps and forearms bulged, and layers of thick flesh rippled down his chest and massive belly. His legs were like small trees. Many men would have thought they were looking at a fat man, and that would have been a mistake.

Ki took in these details with quick flicks of his keen eyes as he watched Da Bao for the telltale twitching of a muscle or a movement of the eyes that would forewarn him of his opponent's first move.

Da Bao's right shoulder dropped a fraction of an inch as he prepared to bring the whip back for a cutting slash. The slight twitch of muscle was all that Ki needed. Holding his body erect, he relaxed the muscles of his legs, bending his knees a fraction of an inch, to give himself the spring he would need. He waited until Da Bao's arm began to move, then leaped sideways. He landed with both feet

71

planted firmly on the whip just as Da Bao began to pull it back.

The Mongolian had not expected to be forced to dislodge Ki. The whip did not move as he'd been sure it would. He yanked at the butt with a sudden application of extra force, but applied it before he'd braced his legs. His own powerful tug pulled the huge man off balance, and for a split second he stood awkwardly, trying to get his equilibrium again.

Ki moved. He leaped toward Da Bao. When his feet left the whip, it was taut in Da Bao's hand, and the foreman staggered back a pace or two. Ki's forward leap took him within range of the Mongolian while he was still off balance. Ki bounced into the air, and as his right foot touched the ground he thrust his left leg out in a powerful sideways kick. Ki's hammerlike foot landed solidly on Da Bao's abdomen, but the layers of muscle shielded the giant's viscera and had no effect other than pushing him back a step.

Ki landed upright, the momentum of his kick still carrying him forward. He swung in a low sweeping *mawashi* kick, with Da Bao's calf as its target, and the force of Ki's kick knocked the man's leg awry. He toppled to the ground.

Da Bao twisted as he fell. He landed with his body quartering Ki's, and landed rolling, his arms stretching out, his big left hand groping for Ki's ankle. Ki had not expected such a quick reaction from such a big man. He'd known, though, that the *mawashi* kick would bring him into dangerously close range of the Mongolian's muscular hands, and known also that he would not be able to reverse his forward momentum in a retreat.

Ki danced forward to avoid Da Bao's groping hand. He broke the rhythm of his move only long enough to administer a heel-strike to the vulnerable few inches of the Mongolian giant's arm, the area just above the elbow, where flexed biceps end and provide no shield of muscle to the sensitive nerves that lie under the shallow layer of flesh. His heel

72

ground into Da Bao's arm, bearing down hard on that small spot, and Da Bao grunted with pain as the nerves twitched and he felt his left forearm and hand begin to grow numb.

Da Bao swung his right arm up and around, the butt of his whip protruding from the heel of his fist. The rough braided leather that covered the rounded end of the butt caught Ki's thigh as he was retreating, and he stumbled forward as his muscles knotted in response to the sudden pain that swept up his thigh from the stabbing blow.

Ki let his momentum carry him out of reach of Da Bao's hands. The time Ki needed to reverse directions and swing back to face his adversary gave Da Bao time to scramble to his feet. The Mongolian still had the butt of the whip firmly in his hand, and his right arm had escaped injury. He brought the butt of the whip forward and back in a lightning-fast sweep, and Ki saw the wicked tuft of iron-tough leather strands that formed the tassel darting toward his face.

There was only one way to escape the swift-moving tassel. Ki dropped to the ground as the tip snapped with the pop of a pistol-shot in the air where his head had been a split-second earlier.

Da Bao's reactions with the whip were faster than his moves in close-quarter combat. He took a step backward as his muscular wrist levered the butt of the whip, keeping it in midair, and began a downward strike that would catch Ki on the ground.

Ki's eyes caught the changed angle of the whip handle. Instead of leaping to his feet and trying to dodge the lash, he stayed on the ground and rolled toward Da Bao. To be effective, the whip had to be used at a distance great enough for its lash to uncurl, and Ki had gotten to within five or six feet of his opponent while the whip was finishing its forward curl.

Da Bao's left arm still dangled limply at his side, and

his right was upraised, holding the butt of the whip, which was just straightening its full length in midair. Ki saw Da Bao brace himself for a kick, and as the giant launched a foot at Ki's rolling form, Ki twisted to avoid the kick.

His quick, squirming twist brought Ki's own feet within striking distance of Da Bao's crotch, and he brought his heel up savagely. He felt his heel grind into Da Bao's testicles and got proof that the kick had hurt the Mongolian badly as Da Bao's right arm sagged and he bent forward, his round face contorted with pain.

Ki rolled to his feet and darted in, accepting the risk that Da Bao would recover quickly enough to sweep him into a crushing bear hug with his uninjured right arm. Da Bao had not begun to bring his body erect when Ki reached him. Ki closed his right hand and brought it down on the back of Da Bao's neck in a smash that landed like a hammer. He felt the resilience of muscle as his fist rebounded, and realized instantly that the heavy hump of shoulder muscle at the base of Da Bao's short neck had absorbed his fist's force and made the blow ineffective.

Da Bao was staggering back from the effects of Ki's smash, but was far from being unable to fight back. While his feet carried him backward away from Ki, the giant raised the butt of the whip and, with a sweep of his hand, brought the supple braided leather snaking back to coil around Ki's waist.

Ki felt the whip wrapping around him and tried to stop, but in his effort to avoid being caught in a bone-crushing hug by the giant's massive arm, he was moving too fast to stop quickly. He grabbed the whip close to his body and used his arm muscles as a brake to slow his momentum and come to a quick stop. Then he began spinning, unwinding himself from the butt end of the whip as its tip continued to coil around his body.

Da Bao was upright now, and saw Ki escaping. He hauled

back hard on the butt of the whip, pulling Ki toward him. As Ki came within striking distance, Da Bao slid his hand up the butt of the whip and raised the heavy bulging end, using it as a club that he brought down in a smash aimed at Ki's head.

Ki blocked the blow with an *age-uki* move, catching the force of the downward smash on his forearm. The blow was a hard one, and Ki's arm muscles began to throb. He saw that he must finish the fight quickly, or the giant Mongolian might outlast him.

A coil or two of the whip still encircled Ki's waist and kept him dangerously close to Da Bao. To gain the time he needed to break free, Ki clenched his hand into a *nakadaka* fist and smashed the foreman's flat nose with the extended knuckle of his middle finger. The blow drew blood, and the giant shook his head angrily when he felt the red stream flowing across his thick lips.

Ki shook himself free of the last coils of the whip and started to step out of Da Bao's reach. Da Bao lurched forward, dropping the whip as he reached to grab Ki. He got a fold of Ki's jacket in his hand and began to pull Ki back toward him.

Ki threw himself backward, yanking the cloth out of the man's grasp, but overbalancing in his effort to break away. He felt himself falling and turned to cushion his fall with his extended hands. As he went down, Ki saw Da Bao lift his foot in a forward step to regain his hold, and with the quick reaction born of many close encounters, he turned his fall not only into an escape but into the beginning of a victory.

As he fell forward, balancing on one leg, Ki straightened his free leg behind him. As Da Bao's foot left the ground, Ki balanced himself on one foot, and when his hands touched the ground he used his muscular forearms as pivots on which to swivel his body. His extended leg caught Da

Bao's knee in a *mawashi* kick, and when the knee bent under the impact, Da Bao lost his balance and fell full-length on the ground.

Ki reached for the whip and his hand closed on it a foot or more above the butt. As he stood erect, Ki wrenched the whip out of Da Bao's hand. He felt for the point where the wooden butt ended and clenched his hands on the inch-thick cylinder, one hand just below the spot where wood and leather met below the braided outer covering, the other an inch or so above the first.

Locking his hands, Ki began twisting. The stout leather resisted, but at the point where Ki was applying all the strength of his well-muscled forearms, the braid was only one layer thick. The tough strips cracked and, once the cracking began, broke quickly. By the time Da Bao had regained his feet, Ki was facing him with a two-foot stick.

Ki brought the fight to a quick end. He feinted to force Da Bao's hands apart, and stabbed the end of the whip-butt into the giant's solar plexus. Even the abnormally thick layer of muscle on Da Bao's abdomen could not shield him from the effects of the jab. His breath escaped in a groaning puff and he tottered forward.

Ki reversed the stick as Da Bao toppled, and administered the coup de grace with another jab. His target for the finishing blow was the temporal bone, just forward of the Mongolian's ear. The blunt end of the whip handle smashed into the giant's skull. Da Bao's lungs had already been emptied by the long groan that followed Ki's first smashing jab. The giant collapsed without a sound and lay in a crumpled heap on the ground at Ki's feet.

From the time Da Bao first raised his whip against Ki until he lay dead, less than two minutes had passed, and Dodds had not moved. He had been glued in place, watching the man he'd thought invincible try to counter Ki's swift, expert moves. Da Bao's defeat left Dodds stunned for a moment, but Jessie had seen Ki in combat often enough to know how quickly the end of the fight would follow its start.

While Dodds was staring at the combatants, Jessie had been preparing for the struggle's end. When it became obvious that Ki was going to be the winner and Dodds was straining forward, his attention focused completely on the fight, Jessie slid her Colt out of her handbag and hid it in a fold of the split riding skirt she'd selected as being more suitable for her visit than jeans or a long formal business skirt.

As Da Bao's head dropped in the climax of his final collapse, Dodds half-turned away from Jessie. She was prepared for his move and raised her Colt. When Dodds turned back, clutching the nickel-plated revolver that he'd drawn, Jessie brought her Colt's barrel down on his gun hand with a quick chopping blow that sent his pistol to the ground. She gave the weapon a kick with her booted toe that sent it skittering out of Dodds's reach.

"I didn't come here to be shot," she snapped. "Or to shoot you, either." She glanced at Ki, who still stood beside Da Bao's body. "It's time for us to go, Ki."

"What about him?" Ki asked, indicating Dodds.

"I won't shoot him in cold blood, you know that," Jessie replied. "Besides, he knows the answers to some questions I want to ask him. Let's go back to his office. We can risk leaving the foreman's body there for a few minutes."

Ki started toward Jessie and Dodds. Jessie waited until he was only a step or two away and motioned for Dodds to walk ahead of them into the office. Not until she'd stepped aside to let Dodds go into the office ahead of them did she realize that she'd underestimated him.

Dodds's counterattack caught Jessie off guard. As he walked past her, he brought his arm around and knocked the muzzle of the Colt aside. The office door was little more

77

than an arm's length away, and Dodds dove through it before she could raise the weapon to fire. As close as Jessie was to the door, Dodds had slammed and locked it by the time she reached it. An instant later he had reached the pull-cord that hung inside the office, and the alarm bell fixed on the wall above the window began clanging loudly.

Ki glanced toward the inner gate. The guard was already running toward them in response to the bell. "Dodds can wait," Ki snapped. "Let's go!"

He picked Jessie up bodily and put her feet-first through the window he'd broken when he dove from the anteroom to face Da Bao. A second later he'd followed her. They ran toward the door that led outside, and got it open just as the guard from the outer gate came running up, drawing his pistol as he ran.

Before the guard could raise his weapon, Ki extended his foot in a sweep that knocked the running man's feet from under him and sent him sprawling facedown, clawing the earth. He and Jessie raced past the prone guard, and as they passed, Ki kicked the man's gun out of reach.

Ki and Jessie reached the fence before the guard regained his feet. Ki drew the bolt and swung the gate open. He opened his pocketknife as they ran down the short path to the dock. They were in the skiff and Ki was slashing the mooring ropes before Dodds and the guards emerged from the gate in pursuit.

Ki planted the tip of the oar against a piling and gave a mighty shove that sent the skiff twenty feet out into the bay just as the first shots from the guards' pistols whistled over their heads.

"We made it!" Jessie gasped.

"Not yet," Ki said soberly while he hauled on the line that pulled up the lugsail. "There might be some rifles around that place, and we're still within rifle range."

A pistol slug slammed into the stern of the skiff, but did not penetrate its thick planking.

"Lie flat on the bottom!" Ki told Jessie, as he adjusted the rigging ropes. "We'll catch the wind now, and if our luck holds good we'll be out of rifle range in a few minutes."

Jessie did not obey. She crouched behind the thwarts and returned the fire of the guards, who were now standing on the end of the dock. The rocking of the skiff spoiled her aim, but her pistol fire sent the men on the dock running back to shore. They stopped there and emptied their revolvers at the moving boat, but without any effect.

By the time the guards had reloaded, the brisk wind sweeping across the bay from the ocean and filled the sail and the boat began making good headway. The guards kept firing, but the bobbing skiff was an uncertain target for even an expert marksman at the distance it had gained while they were reloading their weapons.

When two men with rifles came to join the others, Ki set the skiff on a zigzag course that reduced its speed, but frustrated the riflemen. A few of their shots brought spurts of water up a few feet from the little vessel, but not one of the slugs found its target.

"That was a little close," Ki said, as he and Jessie watched Dodds and his crew walking slowly back to the high gate that enclosed the mill.

"But not as close as some," Jessie reminded him. "And we're very near right now to breaking another limb off the cartel. Maybe tonight at dinner, Eli and Darcy Stone can get us even closer."

★

Chapter 8

"I don't know how Darcy does it," Eli Stone said, pushing his plate away. On his home grounds, he was no longer the testy, imperious person he'd been during the stagecoach ride. "With the little bit of help I can give her, she gets enough news to fill the *Gazette* every week, and still finds time to cook a hot supper most nights. Of course, on Thursday night, when we're printing the paper, we eat at the hotel."

"It was a fine meal," Ki told Darcy. "I enjoyed it."

"So did I," Jessie said. "And it's the first home-cooked meal Ki and I have had since we left the ranch."

"I'd love to see your ranch, Jessie," Darcy sighed. "Even the name sounds romantic, the Circle Star. And after going through a winter on the Oregon coast, I think I'd really enjoy visiting someplace where it's dry and warm."

"We'll arrange a visit," Jessie promised. "I like to spend as much time there as I can."

Eli had gone to a corner cabinet and now hobbled back; in the hand not occupied with his crutch, he balanced a tray on which stood a bottle of Otard cognac and glasses.

"Suppose we go into the parlor and have a sip to settle our dinner," he suggested. "These straight chairs aren't the most comfortable ones for me to sit on with my leg the way it is."

80

By common consent, during dinner they'd avoided any discussion of the burned Starbuck mill, or Dodds, or the big story on which Darcy was working. Both Eli and Darcy had been full of questions about the Circle Star Ranch, and talking about it had made Jessie suddenly homesick for the wide, treeless prairie.

While Eli poured cognac into big snifters, Jessie leaned back against the petit-point upholstery of the rocking chair she'd selected and thought of feeling Sun, her palomino, responding to the touch of her heels with a surge of powerful muscles, and the flow of warm breeze across her face as she galloped home to the sprawling Circle Star ranch house.

She came back to the present with a start when she realized that Eli had repeated a question for the second time.

"I'm sorry, Eli. I'm afraid I was daydreaming," she said.

"I asked whether you want to tell us what you've found out, or whether you want to listen to Darcy first."

"My story's not going to take long to tell," Darcy said. "I've hit a dead end, it seems. I thought I'd guessed who had been telling Tom Buck about Dodds and his mill, but now I'm not sure. One thing *is* sure, though. I'm not giving up."

"What we ran into today, and what Ki found when we were at the mill yesterday afternoon, might help to give you a new starting point," Jessie told them.

With Ki joining her to fill in an occasional bit of detail, Jessie went on to give an abbreviated account of Ki's discovery of the bullet and their encounter with Dodds. When she began to describe the fight between Ki and Da Bao, Darcy broke in.

"Even though I saw what Ki did to those three holdup men who tried to rob the stage, I still don't understand how he could beat them so quickly without a gun," she said. "And what you're saying about him fighting that big Chinese foreman doesn't give me any real idea, either."

81

"You'll have to get Ki to explain, then," Jessie said. "I know a little about *te*, but Ki knows far more than I do."

"It's hard to put into words sometimes," Ki said, frowning.

"Why can't you show us?" Darcy asked. "I mean right now, so father and I can understand what Jessie's telling us."

"If it will help, of course," Ki replied. "But I can't do it alone. I need someone to help me."

"Don't count on me, if there's any moving around to do," Eli said. "I don't want this leg to get banged up again. Darcy, you'll have to take my place."

"You're sure you want to?" Ki asked Darcy. "I'll be very careful, but I might miscalculate and hurt you."

"I'm not as weak and helpless as you might think, Ki," Darcy smiled. "If you hurt me, I'll fight back."

"Stand here in the middle of the room, then," Ki told her. "I'll try to show you as much as I can without finishing the different moves."

Ki found Darcy a very cooperative helper. He was hesitant at first about touching her when he was unable to tell her the exact manner in which to hold her arms and legs. After a few false starts at explaining, she said, "Ki, please stop acting like I'm made out of glass or tissue paper or something else that's delicate. Just take hold of my hands or bend me over or do whatever's necessary to put me in the pose you need. It won't bother me a bit."

Giving the demonstration took much longer than the actual fight had lasted. For each *te* move he'd made, Ki had to pose Darcy in the same positions in which Da Bao had stood, and each time Darcy insisted that he show her the exact point of vulnerability which he'd been attacking.

Ki could not be sure, but as his hands moved over Darcy to apply a carefully limited pressure to a vulnerable spot, he got the impression that she was enjoying the feeling of his hands on her body. When he took her hand to place it on his arm or leg or chest to give her the comparative location of a sensitive nerve complex or a vulnerable area surrounded by muscle, she insisted on exploring the adjacent area to be sure that she was learning the precise point to be attacked.

When they'd finished, Darcy clasped her hands over his and said, "Ki, that was absolutely fascinating! Is there any reason why a woman can't learn this thing you call *te?*"

"None I can think of. It takes a lot of practice, though."

"Can't you show me enough to get me started?"

"I'm sure I can, if you really want to learn."

"Of course I do!" Darcy replied eagerly. "And I'm going to, if you'll just help me!"

After the lengthy demonstration had ended, Jessie made quick work of finishing her story of their escape. She ended by passing on to Eli and Darcy the suspicion she and Ki had of the reason for the secrecy with which Dodds surrounded his operations.

"You've done better in a day than I have in a month!" Darcy exclaimed when Jessie had finished. "I can't believe that Dodds was ready to kill both of you! Aren't you going to have him arrested for attacking you?"

"It would be our word against his," Ki said. "And this is Dodds's home ground. He'd have a dozen witnesses who'd be ready to swear nothing happened. The sheriff, or whoever we'd be telling our story to, would be quicker to believe Dodds than us."

"It's a private fight, Darcy," Jessie added. "It's not the first time we've had to settle problems ourselves."

"We're on your side, of course," Eli promised. "Or you're on ours, I'm not sure which way I ought to put it."

"Let's just say we're together," Jessie suggested.

83

"And—" She stopped when a knock came at the door. "We'll talk about who's on whose side after your guests have gone, Eli."

"It's not guests," Eli said, getting up from his chair. "That knock was at the back door, and we don't bring our guests in through the kitchen."

"Besides, we aren't expecting anyone," Darcy added.

When the knocking was repeated, both Eli and Darcy instinctively looked in the direction of the kitchen. Jessie and Ki exchanged glances without their hosts noticing. Ki pointed to his chest, and Jessie moved her head almost unnoticeably from side to side. She slid her hand under her skirt and took from its garter holster the ugly but effective .41-caliber derringer that she carried when in a town or city. The stubby twin-barreled gun was small enough to be concealed in her palm.

When Eli rose from his chair and reached for his crutch, Jessie stood up also. She said, "I'll go with you, Eli. Some of the problems I mentioned might have followed Ki and me here from the hotel."

"You don't think—" Eli began. He stopped, shook his head, and said, "You may be right, at that. Let's find out."

A lamp still burned in the kitchen. Eli opened the door a crack and looked out. Then he turned to Jessie and said, "There's nothing to worry about, Jessie. It's only our laundryman, Li Yip." Opening the door wider, he said, "Come in, Li. Isn't it pretty late for you to be delivering, though?"

Jessie looked closely at Li Yip. He might have been any age from thirty to fifty. He had on a dark suit and hat; the hat was not creased, and he wore it set squarely on his head. His white shirt was collarless, the neckband fastened with a gold collar button. He stood in the doorway as though uncertain whether or not to enter.

"Please, I don't have laundry, Mr. Stone," Li Yip said.

84

"No? Well, what do you want, then?"

Unexpectedly, Li pointed to Jessie. "The lady here, and the young man who is with her. I was told they would be at your house now. Please, I am sorry I have disturbed you, but I must talk with them."

"Why, that's all right, Li Yip. Come on in and talk."

Li shook his head. "No, please, Mr. Stone. I cannot now come in. But if we can talk here..." He looked questioningly at Jessie. "You do not mind if we stay here to talk?"

"I don't mind a bit. What do you want to talk about?"

"Please, not yet. The man called Ki, he is here?"

"Yes." Jessie raised her voice and called, "Ki. Will you come here? The visitor is looking for us."

Ki came into the kitchen, followed by Darcy.

"Li Yip?" Darcy said. "We don't have any laundry—"

"Li's not delivering, Darcy," Eli said. "He came to talk to Jessie and Ki."

"What on earth for?" she asked.

"Looks like we'll have to wait until Li tells us." Eli turned back to the Chinese and said, "Well, Li, now that Ki's here, go ahead."

Li Yip faced Ki and said a few words in Chinese. Ki shook his head, and replied with a short spurt of Japanese. This time it was Li who shook his head.

"We'll talk in English, then," Ki said.

"What language we talk does not matter," Li said. Looking at Ki, he went on, "One of my countrymen came to me today. He is not only a countryman, but a *tong* brother."

"He must be the man the foreman was beating!" Jessie said quickly.

Li Yip nodded. "He has asked me to speak for him. He has no English." Turning back to Ki, he asked, "You please will talk to him? I will interpret for you."

"Of course I'll talk with him," Ki said. "Where is he?"

Li Yip pointed to the black shadow cast by the fence that encircled the yard. "He is waiting there. He was afraid that someone would see him."

"Well, bring him in," Eli told the laundryman.

Pointing to the lamp, Li said, "Please, you will blow it out?"

"I'll pull the window shades down," Darcy volunteered. "That will be better than talking in the dark."

"I will get Yu Gar and bring him in, then," Li said.

He walked across the yard and disappeared in the black shadow of the fence. Darcy drew the window shade to the bottom and went into the front of the house to attend to the rest of the windows.

Li Yip returned almost at once, followed by the coolie who had been the object of Da Bao's attack at the mill earlier in the day. Yu Gar still wore the shapeless blue cotton trousers and jacket he'd had on then, but they had been washed. A bandage circled his head.

He looked around, his mouth pursed and his eyes darting from one to the other of those in the room, until he saw Ki. Rushing to Ki, Yu Gar dropped to his knees. He grasped Ki's hand and pressed his head to the back of it, and said something in his native language. Ki looked questioningly at Li Yip.

"Yu Gar says he owes you his life," Li translated. "He has no money with which to redeem it from you, but he will stay with you and serve you well until you tell him that he has paid his debt to you."

"Wait, now!" Ki protested. He tried to pull his hand away, but Yu Gar clung to it tightly. Ki went on, "Yu Gar doesn't owe me anything. I didn't help him for his own sake, but because Dodds is as much an enemy of Jessie and me as he is of—" Ki broke off and shook his head. "I can't explain it so he'll understand. Jessie, how can I get out of this?"

In spite of the complexity of the situation in which Ki found himself, Jessie could not suppress a smile. She told Ki, "I think perhaps you'd consider Yu Gar's debt paid if he gave us some information, Ki. There are a lot of things I'd like to know about that mill of Dodds's. But don't refuse his gift just yet. You'd hurt his feelings. He's offering you the only thing of value that he has."

Li Yip looked at Jessie and nodded. "You have wisdom more than your years, Miss Starbuck. Let me judge how much of what you have said I will tell Yu Gar."

"It looks like this is going to take some time to settle," Eli Stone broke in. "I think we'd better go in the parlor where we can all sit down and be comfortable."

"You do us honor, Mr. Stone," Li Yip said, bowing solemnly to Eli. "I will explain to Yu what we are to do." He went to where Yu Gar still knelt in front of Ki, put his hand on the coolie's shoulder, and said a few words in Chinese. Yu Gar shook his head as he replied in the same tongue, and for a few moments the two talked in rapid bursts. Finally, Yu Gar released Ki's hand and rose to his feet.

"He is still afraid he will be seen," Li Yip explained. "He has run away from the mill, and if his owner finds him, Yu Gar is sure he will be killed."

"You mean Dodds *owns* him?" Jessie asked, her voice showing the shock and surprise she felt.

Li Yip said, "Mr. Dodds owns all my countrymen who work for him, Miss Starbuck."

"But that's against the law!" Jessie exclaimed. She paused and went on, "But I suppose that wouldn't mean anything to Dodds." Then, silently, she added, *Or to the men behind him*. Looking at Ki, she saw from his raised eyebrows and questioning look that he'd caught her unspoken thought.

When the group had settled in the parlor, Yu Gar began

to talk. Li Yip stopped him at the end of each few sentences to translate what was to those listening a story of human slavery, not very different from that which most of those present thought had been ended by the Civil War.

Yu's story was not long. He had been sold as an infant to a Chinese warlord, and trained as a household servant. When his owner had been killed in one of the dynastic wars that had kept China torn up for almost a century, he had been resold to a slaver and brought to the United States, smuggled ashore at Fogarty Bay, and put to work in the lumber mill. Kept in a barracks on the grounds of the mill, Yu Gar and his fellow slaves had been bossed by Da Bao and two other equally brutal foremen, and kept prisoner by the armed guards patrolling the fences.

"But Yu knew that he would be blamed for causing Da Bao to be killed," Li Yip explained, then added, addressing Ki, "Since you had befriended him once, he came to me, looking for help in finding you."

"How did Yu Gar know where to find you, Li?" Darcy asked.

Li Yip hesitated for a long while before he replied. Then he said, "Miss Darcy, I can answer your question only at the risk of my life."

"Whatever you tell us won't be repeated outside this room, Li," Eli promised. "And if you tell us what has been going on up at Dodds's mill, it'll help us to stop it mighty fast."

Li Yip nodded. "I know that, Mr. Stone. Information I gave Tom Buck, he has been passing on to Miss Darcy. And now Yu Gar has brought me more important news than any I ever gave to Tom."

"And you're the one who's been telling Tom all the things he passed on to me!" Darcy exclaimed. "I didn't even think of you as being Tom's source of inside information!"

"Confucius has written that virtue is to love men and

wisdom is to understand men, Miss Darcy," Li Yip replied. "I love my countrymen and have tried to help them, but as I also understand that Dodds is an evil man, I believed it wise to let no one know I was doing so. Since Tom died, I have thought more than once that I should tell you, Miss Darcy, but I—well, it shames me to say this, but I have been afraid, just as Yu Gar is now."

"Tom told me that he was looking for more news, the last time I talked to him before he died," Darcy said.

"Yu Gar was not sure before. Now he knows much more."

"Much more about what?"

"About the murders and what has happened after them."

"Murders?" Eli exclaimed. "Tom didn't mention that."

"I did not tell him because I had no proof. But even without proof, I must tell you of them now so that you will understand what will happen soon."

"Go on, Li Yip," Darcy said. "If you can tell me enough about how and when and where Dodds murdered someone, I'll find a way to prove he did it."

Li Yip shook his head. "I think it is not possible to find proof, Miss Darcy. The bodies were taken to sea and put in the water. And the only witness whose name I know is dead."

"Who was that?" Jessie asked. "Not Tom, I hope."

"No, no!" Li replied. "It was Da Bao, the man Ki killed."

"If I'd known he could have helped convict Dodds of murder, I would have spared his life," Ki said.

"That would not have mattered," Li Yip assured him. "Da Bao would have said nothing against Dodds. You see, Dodds watched Da Bao murder the women."

"Women?" Stone asked. "What women, Li?"

Li Yip was silent for a long moment, then he said hesitantly, "It is not a nice thing I must tell you. I do not know whether I should speak of such things before Miss Darcy and your guest, Mr. Stone."

Jessie and Darcy spoke at the same time, their voices mingling in a babble no one could understand. They stopped, and Darcy nodded to Jessie to speak first.

"You won't shock us, whatever it is you have to say, Mr. Li. Go on and tell your story."

"I say the same thing," Darcy nodded.

"Very well," Li said. "You must understand first that my countrymen do not like any woman who is not of our race to—" he stopped, made a false start, and stopped again.

"Mr. Li," Jessie said, "I have a feeling that you're afraid you'll embarrass us. Now, Darcy and I are both old enough to know that men and women go to bed together to enjoy each other. If that's part of your story, I've told it for you, so go on."

"Thank you," Li said. "You have made it easy. It is a thing I did not wish to mention, but the men of China wish to enjoy only women of China. Dodds brought women to the mill to keep his slaves satisfied."

"Prostitutes," Jessie said.

"Whores," Darcy blurted at the same time.

"Yes," Li nodded. "They have their own quarters, and each of Dodds's slaves is given a time to visit them. Yu Gar was fond of a certain one of these women, and a short time ago, she disappeared. He asked the others where she had gone, but they did not tell him. Then one of them let slip that the woman Yu asked about had been killed, as well as two others, in a—" He frowned and went on, "I do not know the English word . . ."

"Orgy?" Eli suggested.

"Yes. Dodds came to their quarters drunk, early one morning when none of the men would be there. How he killed the woman I do not exactly know, but two others knew of what he had done. Dodds then ordered Da Bao to kill them too, so there would be no one to appear as a witness if his crime should be discovered."

"Let me guess the rest, Li," Ki said. "Before Da Bao could kill them, the women had told some of the others, and it was one of those who told Yu Gar what had happened."

"You are correct, Ki," Li said.

Ki turned to Jessie. "It looks like we've got Dodds, then."

"There's only one thing you're overlooking, Ki," she replied. "Calling Dodds a murderer is one thing. Proving it in court without witnesses is quite another."

★

Chapter 9

Ki was silent for a moment, then he said, "You're right, of course, Jessie. It slipped my mind for a moment that we have no witnesses to offer a court. And I'm partly to blame for that."

"I wasn't suggesting it's your fault, Ki," Jessie said.

"Of course not. But I did kill Da Bao," Ki replied.

"We have no witnesses to Tom Buck's murder, either," she pointed out. "And while Dodds may not have pulled the trigger of the gun that killed Tom, all of us know he ordered him killed."

"Please." Li Yip's tone was almost apologetic. In their discussion, they'd almost forgotten the two Chinese. All of them looked expectantly at Li. He went on, "I know the keeping of my countrymen as slaves is a crime for which Dodds can be tried."

"Of course it is, Li," Eli replied. "But—" He stopped suddenly and pressed his lips together.

Li said quickly, "Do not try to spare me embarrassment, Mr. Stone. I understand that my countrymen's testimony is valued very little in your courts."

"I'm afraid that's right, Li," Darcy agreed.

"This is a fact I learned from Tom Buck," Li went on. "It was his idea that I ask the men Dodds holds as slaves to give me information about crimes Dodds had committed, or evil things he was about to do."

"How could you get that kind of information?" Darcy asked.

"Slaves have eyes and ears," Li replied. "And in pillow-talk with women, men speak unguarded words. Walls will hold prisoners, but cannot stop their messages from passing through."

"So you're the one who was giving Tom the information he passed on to me," Darcy said thoughtfully.

Li nodded. "He said that if he could learn of Dodds's plans, he would then furnish witnesses who have the trust of your judges and juries, people to whom they would listen. Witnesses such as yourself, Miss Darcy."

"You mean—" Darcy began indignantly, then she stopped and smiled. "I'd be obliged to testify, wouldn't I, if Tom had lived long enough to do what he'd promised, and given me information that would have let me actually see Dodds breaking the law." She thought for a moment and added, "It would be a fair exchange for a good news story, I suppose."

"That is why I brought Yu Gar here," Li said. "He knows of something Dodds has been planning that will give you just such a story as you speak of."

"Something that hasn't yet happened?" Eli frowned.

"Yes, Mr. Stone," Li nodded. "But something that will take place very soon now."

"Can you tell me what it is?" Darcy asked eagerly.

"Of course," Li answered, his tone so casual that he might have been replying to a question about the time of day. "I have told you of the women who were murdered. To replace them, Dodds ordered more of their kind from China. Not three, but many. Ten at least, perhaps even more."

93

"If you can prove it's Dodds who is bringing in those women, you'll be able to put him in jail for several years," Jessie told Darcy. "For holding them in slavery and for violating Oregon's Exclusion Act."

"It's too bad they're not violating a federal law," Ki said thoughtfully. "You could get some help from your friend Marshal Long, Jessie, if a federal law was being broken."

"Yes. But even if Longarm can't help, I'm sure the Oregon attorney general would be interested." She turned to Eli. "How well-connected are you in Salem?"

"Enough to pull whatever strings are necessary," the editor replied. "I've done a few favors for the attorney general, and the *Gazette* has always supported him at election time. If I asked him to send an investigator to Baytown on a case like this, he'd do it."

"It looks to me as if Li Yip has brought us the kind of case that would put Dodds away for quite a while," Jessie said.

"It does, at that," Ki agreed. He asked Li Yip, "Are these women going to arrive soon?"

"Very soon. Within a few days."

"How do you know?" Jessie asked.

"Because Dodds received yesterday a letter that came on the steamship from Yokohama. It said that the ship on which the new women are being sent left Shanghai one month ago."

"Why did the message come from Yokohama if the ship sailed from Shanghai?" Ki asked.

"I regret to say, Ki, that the ship belongs to a Japanese," Li replied apologetically.

Ki said quickly, "That does not surprise me or embarrass me, Li Yip. I know there are as many cruel and heartless Japanese as there are of any other race."

"If I understand this, Li Yip, the women are on a sailing vessel, and the steamship with the letter got here first because it's so much faster. Is that right?" Jessie asked.

"That is so, Miss Starbuck."

"A month's about what a vessel under sail would need to get here," Eli said. "Give or take a few days either way."

"That means the women could get here anytime, then!" Darcy exclaimed. "If I want to get a really good story, we'll have to move fast!" She thought for a moment. "Father, can we get a man from the attorney general's office here in time?"

"If I can get word to him right away, we can." Eli grunted sourly and added, "The trouble is, nobody can depend on the cussed U.S. Mail anymore. It takes three or four days for a letter to get sixty miles to Salem."

Li Yip said, "My cousin, Li On, leaves for Salem tonight in his cart, to buy fresh vegetables for his store. He will be there by noon tomorrow. He can take your letter, Mr. Stone."

Stone wasted no time. He said, "Darcy, bring me my lap-desk and I'll write the letter this minute."

Jessie asked Li Yip, "Do you know where the ship bringing these women will land?"

Li exchanged a few words with Yu Gar and told Jessie, "At the loading dock at Dodds's mill. Yu Gar says it will stay offshore until dark, and put in at the dock after the mill has closed down for the night."

"So unless the ship gets here late in the day, we'll have a few hours to get ready," Jessie said, as much to herself as to the others, then said to Ki, "We must find someone we can hire to watch from the spit and warn us when the Japanese ship arrives. Amos Weatherby will know of a good man, I'm sure."

Ki contented himself with a nod, for, just as Jessie finished speaking, Eli Stone looked up and said, "That ought to get the old boy into action!"

He folded the letter he'd written and put it in an envelope

on which he wrote the attorney general's name in his bold script. He held the letter out and Li Yip stepped over and took it.

"I must go, if there are no more questions you wish to ask me," he told Stone. "Li On will be leaving soon."

"If we want to know anything, Li, one of us will stop by the laundry," Darcy said. "You have a place there where Yu Gar can stay, I'm sure."

"Yes, Miss Darcy. He will be safe."

"Then, as soon as we've made some more plans, we'll arrange for all of us to meet again and talk them over," Eli said.

When the two Chinese had left, Darcy said, "I hope that Japanese ship doesn't get here until we're ready!"

"What do you mean by ready?" Ki asked her. "A small boat can sail from Baytown to Dodds's mill in an hour, and all we need to do is to be where we can watch the women brought ashore."

"I want to do more than watch, Ki," Darcy replied. "You remember the plates I brought back from Salem on the stage?"

"Yes, but what does chinaware have to do with this?"

"They're not china plates. They're photographic plates, a new kind called dry plates. Tom Buck told me about them."

"I still don't understand, unless you expect to take pictures of the women coming ashore," Ki said.

"That's exactly what I want to do, Ki!" Darcy replied. "And I can, with these new plates. Instead of exposing them for ten seconds, I can get a picture with the lens open for only one second. And these plates don't have to be soaked in silver nitrate just before I take a picture, so I can carry a lot of them and take all the pictures I want, instead of only one or two."

"Pictures would certainly be conclusive evidence," Jessie

said. "But wouldn't you have to get dangerously close to the slave ship to take them?"

"And how will you take pictures at night, even if these new dry plates are as good as you say they are?" Ki asked.

Darcy started to answer Ki before the full meaning of his question struck her, and she sat staring for a moment with her mouth open. Then she snapped her firm jaw shut and said with determination, "I don't know, Ki. But I'll think of something! I'm not going to give up the idea of taking pictures!"

"Don't forget you've got magnesium powder," Eli said.

"I haven't forgotten. But you know the trouble with magnesium powder, Father. When I use it outdoors, the wind blows it out of the flash tray before I can trip the shutter."

"I like the idea of having pictures that can be shown the jury at a trial, though," Jessie said. "I want to see Dodds convicted, and I'm in favor of anything that will help put him in prison for a long time. Let's think about it, Darcy, maybe we can come up with an idea."

"I haven't forgotten my earlier idea, either, that I'd like to learn about *te,*" Darcy said. She looked at Ki. "It's just a little after nine o'clock, Ki. Do you feel like teaching me a little bit tonight?"

"Of course I do, Darcy," he replied.

"Now wait a minute!" Eli said. "This parlor's no place for you and Ki to start jumping and doing a lot of kicking and throwing your arms around."

"Eli's right, Darcy," Ki agreed. "We do need more open space to work in."

"I know just the place!" Darcy said. "The *Gazette* office. We've got a big back room there where we store paper, and it's almost empty now, because we're almost down to our reserve supply and won't get our next shipment for two or three weeks. Let's go there, Ki. Jessie and Father can talk about our plans while you give me my first lesson."

Jessie said, "If Eli will excuse me, I think I'll say good night now and walk as far as the newspaper office with you and Ki, then go on to the hotel. We had a very busy day yesterday, and I'm about ready for bed."

"I don't mind a bit, Jessie," Eli told her. "When Darcy gets a bee in her bonnet, she doesn't pay any attention to what time of day it is. Besides, I need to stretch and get the kinks out of my bad leg."

As the trio walked through Baytown's silent streets, deserted even at that early hour, Jessie said to Darcy, "I've gotten the impression that those Chinese coolies Dodds uses as slaves interest you more than just as the subject of a newspaper story. Do you mind telling me why?"

"I suppose I'm just interested in people being free, Jessie. Maybe I get it from my Aunt Lucy. You've probably heard of her. She's been holding women's-rights conventions every year, to make women people in their own right, instead of just slaves to men."

"Lucy Stone is your aunt?" Jessie exclaimed. "Of course I've heard of her. She's created quite a stir in the East for a long time."

"Well, don't you agree with her?" Darcy asked.

"Of course I do. But I suppose I've really been lucky. My father decided that he wouldn't marry again after my mother died, so he brought me up with the idea that I'd take over his estate and run the businesses he'd started or bought. He was murdered before he taught me as much as I'd like to know, but I haven't had any trouble being my own person."

"My father's treating me the same way," Darcy said. "But I guess you've noticed that."

"Yes. Perhaps that's why we get along so well, we think quite a bit alike. Even Ki, who comes from a place where

98

women aren't really considered people, agrees that the men in his country are wrong in the way they treat their wives."

"I've seen how bad it is," Ki said soberly. "But even if I do agree with you and Jessie, Darcy, it's something I don't like to talk about."

"We'll talk about *te*, then," Darcy said as they stopped in front of the *Gazette* office and she fumbled in her purse for her key. "Do you want to walk with Jessie to the hotel and come back, Ki? It's just around the corner."

"After our talk about women being independent, I'd feel like a fool needing an escort to go such a short way," Jessie smiled. "You two go on with your lesson. I'll be quite all right."

Breathing deeply of the cool wind that came briskly off the bay, Jessie took her time covering the short distance to the hotel. The streets were even darker and quieter than they had been when she and Ki had gone to the Stone residence earlier.

When Jessie entered the small lobby, the clerk at the registration desk was nowhere in sight, so she followed the custom that prevailed in all small-town hotels of the day. Going behind the desk, she took out the key to her room and mounted the flight of stairs to the second floor.

Not even a sound of snoring broke the silence of the dimly lighted corridor. Unlocking the door of her room, Jessie swung open the door and had started to step inside when her sixth sense suddenly flashed a warning. Belatedly, she remembered that she'd left a lamp turned low on the dresser. The room was now pitch-dark.

Jessie threw herself backward, trying to stop in midstride, but her half-completed step had carried her into the doorway. She still had one hand on the doorknob when the door was suddenly yanked wide. Too startled to release the knob in time, Jessie was pulled forward and the incomplete step became a forward lurch that dragged her into the darkened room. Rough hands closed around her mouth and right wrist.

Jessie got a fleeting glimpse of shadowy figures moving in the almost impenetrable gloom as other hands grasped her. One of the hands covered her mouth just as she was opening it to scream, and another hand caught the arm that had been yanked forward by the door.

Wriggling in her captor's grasp, Jessie kicked at random until she felt the toe of her shoe meet something solid, and one of the men holding her gave a grunt of pain. She kept kicking, and writhed her firmly muscled body, trying to pull her arms free. The two men holding her were both big and strong, and she could not break their holds.

"Shut that damn door!" one of them said. "This bitch is fighting like a wildcat, and we'll have to strike a light to see how to tie her up!"

"Shut it yourself!" the second man snapped. "You're closer to it than I am!"

After a moment the door was kicked closed, but Jessie did not stop her struggle. She made her efforts convincing, knowing that she had no real hope of freeing herself, but working toward the ruse that she now tried. She suddenly relaxed her tensed muscles, hoping that when her captors felt her go limp, they would conclude she was giving up and ease their grip, giving her a fresh chance to break free.

This pair did not take the bait. They tightened their holds instead, and Jessie realized that she must not renew her efforts, but must save her strength for a fresh try later on. She did not fight back as the two dragged her to the dresser and one of them removed the arm he'd clamped around her body while he struck a match and lighted the lamp.

Now Jessie could see the two men in the mirror. She looked at them closely before they pushed her roughly to the floor, facedown. One of them put a knee in the small of her back and pinned her firmly in place. The brief glimpse Jessie had gotten of the faces of her assailants told her that neither of the men had been among the guards with whom she and Ki had fought earlier in the day at the mill, though Jessie had no doubt that the men had been sent by Dodds.

"Grab this hand," one of them said. "Hold it while I get out the rope."

Jessie, unable to breathe freely because of the smothering hand that was still clamped over her mouth, and pinned to the floor by the knee of one of the men, did not struggle as her wrists were bound. She concentrated all the strength she could muster in doubling her fists to flex the muscles in her wrists and spread the bases of her thumbs as Ki had taught her to do, tensing every muscle in her arms to keep the bonds from being pulled completely taut.

Later, when she let the tension relax, there would be a tiny bit of play in the rope. Only after the man who'd tied her up pulled a strip of cloth through her lips and tied the gag at the back of her neck before standing up did Jessie let the tension in her arms and wrists relax.

"All right," the man who seemed to be the leader said. "We didn't make much noise, but let's get the hell outta here. That damn chink that travels with her might be along any time, and I sure don't aim to tangle with him after what he done to Da Bao."

"Listen," the second man said, "we ain't in no hurry to get the dame to the mill, are we? There's a good bed over there, and I'd like a piece of white woman's ass for a change."

"She'd be all right, I guess." The second man rubbed his hand over Jessie's firm breasts and down her abdomen. "Feels good. But we got orders not to mess around with her."

"Ah, nobody's gonna know!"

"She'd know, and I bet sure as hell she'd tell, too."

"Well, shit! If we ain't gonna fuck her, go on and tie her feet. She can kick like a jackass. She sure landed a couple of good ones on me."

"Tie her feet, hell! How're we gonna get her down to the bay if she can't walk?"

"I sorta figured we'd carry her."

"And what if somebody seen us on the street?"

"Hell, it ain't far! Besides, we sure didn't see nobody walking around when we come up here."

"Ah, shut up, and let's move! I say she walks, so that's how it's gonna be!"

Jessie neither resisted her captors nor cooperated with them. She let them lift her, and when one of the men got on each side of her and took hold of her upper arms, she refused to move her feet as they started forward, but remained passive and let them drag her across the floor.

"Lift them feet and walk, you bitch!" the leader snarled. When Jessie did not obey after they'd taken another step or two across the room, he said, "Shit! Pick her up and let her feet dangle. Nobody's going to notice."

Suspended between the two men, Jessie was borne out of the room, along the corridor, through the still-deserted lobby, and out to the street. She realized then that the men must have disposed of the room clerk in some fashion in order to carry out their scheme. As the pair bore her along the deserted street toward the dock, she hoped they would encounter someone who would see her plight and raise an alarm, but her hope was in vain.

They reached the dock, and Jessie's hopes rose again when she saw lights still showing through the portholes of two of the trawlers and the small schooner that had been moored there earlier in the day.

No one was on the decks of any of the boats, and there was no one on the wharf. The men carried Jessie to its farthest end, where a lugger a bit larger than the one she and Ki had rented was moored a little apart from the other vessels.

Unceremoniously the two men dumped Jessie into the vessel and left her lying on the duckboards while they cast off the mooring ropes and pushed the vessel out into Fogarty Bay. They hauled up the sail. It filled quickly in the brisk breeze. The lugger gained headway and the man at the tiller set it on a northward course, toward Dodds's mill.

★

Chapter 10

Ki watched Jessie until she turned the corner of the street leading to the hotel, then followed Darcy inside the newspaper office. A night light at the rear of the big room shed a dim glow on the desks that stood just inside the door, on the stone-topped makeup slabs that took up most of the space beyond them, on the cases of type that lined the walls, and on the Hoe flatbed press that occupied the rear part of the building.

Darcy picked up a sheet of copy paper from one of the desks as they passed, and rolled it into a long thin spill as she led Ki to a door behind the press. She held the spill above the chimney of the night light until it ignited, and used it to light their way into the storage room, where she touched its flaming end to the wick of the lamp that stood on a small table just inside the door. Along the back wall, flat brown-wrapped packages of newsprint rose in tiers like stairs to the ceiling, but except for these and the table holding the lamp, the big room was empty.

Darcy ground out the spill carefully, being sure no small spark remained on its tip. Then she laid her purse beside the lamp, took off her hat, and placed it on top of the purse. Running her fingers through the tight curls of her auburn hair, she turned to face Ki.

"Well?" she asked. "Will we have space enough here?"

"More than enough. For your first lesson or two, we won't need much space, but you'll need a lot of patience, Darcy."

"What must I learn first, Ki?"

"Before you can use *te*, you must know where there are nerves and other vulnerable points that you can attack. After you've learned them, we'll go on to the moves you'll use."

"I'm willing to learn. How do we start?"

"We start with you taking off your shoes." Ki was slipping his own shoes off, and as he spoke he began untying the sash that drew his loose jacket in at the waist. "I'll take off my jacket so I can show you the points on my own body and on yours. If you're not bashful, it will help if you take off your skirt and blouse, too."

"You heard what I told Jessie, Ki. If it's all right for a man to show his body, a woman should be able to show hers as well, without being bashful or self-conscious about it."

Ki pulled his loose jacket over his head. Darcy had been looking down at her feet while she levered out of her low-cut pumps. She raised her eyes and saw the layers of muscle that rippled smoothly under Ki's bare skin as he moved, the bulging of his well-developed biceps, and the thick cords of muscle that extended down his forearms. Involuntarily she drew a short, sharp breath, and her eyes widened.

Darcy unfastened the snaps that cinched her skirt in at the waist and let it slide to the floor. She unbuttoned her blouse, shrugged it off her shoulders, and dropped it on top of the skirt. In the soft lamplight her bare shoulders gleamed with the luster of ivory that has been carefully buffed and polished. Her slip was fashioned with a low vee neckline that let Ki see the first swelling of her high full breasts and the dusky shadowed cleft between them.

"Will this be all right?" she asked Ki.

"It will do for now."

"If my slip's going to be in the way, I can take it off too," she offered. Before Ki could reply, Darcy shrugged and went on, "It'll be easier to take it off now than later." Suiting actions to her words, she drew the straps of the slip over her shoulders and let it ripple down her body to join the blouse and skirt. Her camisole was cut lower than the slip, and bared the upper bulge of her breasts. Ki could see the rosettes of her breasts pushing like small fingertips against the fabric, and her dark pubic hair outlined beneath the taut white cloth of her knee-length pantalettes. She said, "Now. I'm ready to begin."

"Yes," Ki nodded. He stepped up to her and took her right hand. "First you must learn to use your fingers, Darcy. Use them as you would a spear, keeping your hand stiff."

As he spoke, Ki was holding her palm against his, pressing with his thumb against the back of her hand. When her hand was flat and stiff, he folded her thumb under the palm.

"With your fingertips, you stab into a spot where there are nerves close below the skin. Like this."

Ki pulled Darcy's fingertips into his neck below the point of his jaw, then into his Adam's apple, and finally into his solar plexus.

"Why couldn't I just hit those places with my fist?" Darcy asked after he'd gone over the sensitive spots several times to make sure that she could locate them accurately.

"A fist is too blunt," Ki told her. "The force of your blow is spread over too wide an area. You must stab with your fingers stiff, as though they were a blade. Let me show you."

Clenching his hand into a fist, Ki tapped her abdomen with a gentle blow. Then he flattened his hand and jabbed the same spot. He controlled the force of the blow carefully, but Darcy winced when his iron-hard fingertips sank into her soft skin.

"Ouch!" she exclaimed.

"I'm sorry," Ki apologized. "I wasn't trying to hurt you."

"It didn't really hurt," she smiled. "But I was surprised to find how much I felt it." She rubbed her palm over Ki's flat, muscled belly. "Even if I hit you that way with all my strength, I don't think I'd make much of a dent in your stomach, Ki. It's as hard as marble."

"I work to keep it that way," Ki said. He was very aware of Darcy's warm flesh on his.

Darcy slid her hand from Ki's abdomen up his chest, and felt his upper arm. She tried to sink her fingertips into his biceps, but Ki clenched his fist to tighten the muscle, and her fingertips only dimpled his skin.

"Your arm's even harder than your stomach," she said, her eyes fixed on his. She ran her hand down his side and to his crotch, found his flaccid shaft, and closed her fingers around it. "But you're not hard where it counts." She squeezed him with a gently tugging caress and asked, "Can you make it hard for me, Ki?"

"Of course, if you're sure you'd like for me to."

"You know that I would. I don't think I've fooled you a bit with my interest in *te*. You must've known from the way I was so anxious to shed my clothes that it was only an excuse to get us here alone together."

"It did occur to me that you had more than *te* in mind."

Ki relaxed his control enough to let himself swell into the beginning of an erection. He bent to press his lips in the hollow of Darcy's throat, and then kissed his way up the pulsing column of her neck. Her hand closed tighter on his erection and she ground her breasts into the hard muscles of his chest.

Ki found the snaps of her camisole and undid them, and pulled the thin garment away so that they stood flesh to flesh. Darcy moved her torso from side to side, rubbing her hardened nipples across his smooth skin.

"You're not getting hard very fast," she said, her voice

puzzled. "Do you need me to help you come up?"

"No." Ki allowed himself to stiffen a bit more and Darcy gasped as she felt him swell in a sudden surge. "But there's no need for us to hurry. Pleasure deferred is all the sweeter when it is finally realized."

Darcy released one hand and began pushing the waist-band of Ki's trousers down on his hips. Her fingers found the buttons of the fly and freed them.

When her soft hands returned to his crotch and began caressing him again, Ki let himself become fully erect. Darcy gasped as she felt his response to her urgent fingering, and when Ki began caressing the tips of her breasts with his lips and tongue, she pulled his member between her thighs and closed them on him while her hips began working back and forth.

Ki sensed the urgency of Darcy's need. Without inter-rupting the caresses he was bestowing on her breasts, he undid the drawstring of her pantalettes and slipped them down her hips. Darcy clung to him as Ki pushed the pan-talettes lower, and clung even tighter as he tried to twist away from her so that he could to part their bodies and shove the tightly-fitting undergarment down her thighs.

When Darcy realized why Ki was pulling away, she broke their embrace and kicked off the clinging pantalettes. Looking down at his jutting erection, she gasped, "Hurry, Ki! I've deferred that pleasure you were talking about just as long as I can!"

Ki lifted Darcy by the waist and she clasped her hands behind his neck. Her thighs were spread, and Ki lowered her to straddle his shaft. Darcy squirmed, trying to bring her hips up and take him inside, but Ki began to move his own hips slowly back and forth. Darcy shuddered gently as she felt him rubbing against the moist softness of the lips between her thighs. She sighed happily as she brought her

108

legs together and clamped his erection tightly in the soft wet flesh between them.

Her lips sought Ki's, and her tongue snaked into his mouth, seeking his. She squeezed her thighs together more tightly as he continued to rub his shaft gently in the cradling warmth of her smooth skin. She groaned softly deep in her throat, a wordless humming that increased in volume until its rhythm began to break and her tongue darted deeper into Ki's mouth.

A quivering took Darcy's body. She clung tighter as the quivering grew in its intensity. Then her head jerked back, breaking their kiss, and her body shook in Ki's hands. Darcy tried to push down harder on his erection, but Ki held her firmly while she shook and cried in soft whimpers, and he felt the warmth of her juices flowing around his engorged sex. The spasm lasted only a few seconds. Darcy opened her eyes and looked into Ki's.

"That was nice, Ki, but it wasn't enough," she whispered. "I feel good, but I know you can make me feel better. You still aren't inside me, and that's what I want."

"I know. But it is just the beginning of our pleasure, Darcy. There will be more, I promise you."

Darcy's body had stopped quivering now. Her hands were still locked around his neck, and Ki held her to him with one arm embracing her waist while he slid first one arm and then the other under her thighs.

Darcy's knees were around Ki's elbows, her thighs spread wide. She looked down between their bodies and saw his sex standing firm and high. With a deep, expectant inhalation, she slid one hand between their bodies and guided him into her. Ki brought his hips forward and thrust into her, but shallowly. Darcy gasped, a deep sighing inhalation.

"Go deeper, Ki!" she urged, trying to pull her buttocks

forward but unable to do so. "I'm burning up inside! Go in all the way!"

Stretching his arms, Ki clasped his hands behind Darcy's hips and pulled her softly quivering buttocks to him while he thrust. She cried out, a small throaty scream in which pain and pleasure mingled as Ki drove in.

"Oh, yes!" Darcy gasped. "You're in me now the way I want you!"

Ki did not reply. Darcy's eyes had been squeezed tightly closed in the ecstasy of Ki's deep lunge. She opened them now and looked into his questioningly.

"You won't have to wait," he said. "Our pleasure's been deferred enough for us to enjoy it together now."

Still holding her impaled on him, he took a step toward the stacks of newsprint and stepped up to stand on the bottom tier. Darcy looked around to see what he was doing, then relaxed while Ki sank to his knees, lowering her to lie on the smooth hard surface, her knees still locked around his elbows, her thighs sprawled wide, her buttocks raised.

"Ooh!" she moaned. "If you only knew how I feel, you'd hurry, Ki! I'm holding back, but I'm just about ready again!"

"Don't hold back," Ki told her, raising himself and driving into her with a swift, full penetration. "Give yourself to pleasure, now!"

Darcy's answer was a small stifled cry as Ki pounded into her. The cries came faster and closer together as he drove with full, steady strokes. She reached her climax quickly, moaning and shaking through its peak, and her body went limp as the spasms rippled through it and stopped, but Ki did not stop.

He kept up his measured stroking until Darcy grew tense again. When she began to cry out once more as she ap-praoched the almost unendurable peak of pleasure, Ki released his control and let his own climax began. He held himself back once, to let Darcy meet him, and when her

110

inarticulate cries grew loud in his ears, Ki spurted into her with a deep final thrust, while, beneath him, Darcy writhed and moaned until they both went limp and lay quiet.

Ki moved first. He raised himself and, with his hands flat on the brown-wrapped paper shelf, braced his arms stiffly at full length and looked down at Darcy. Her dark red curls were plastered to her forehead. She still had her eyes closed, and her lips wore a smile of contented satiety. Then her eyes opened and she looked up at him and her smile grew wider.

"I know what you mean now by pleasure deferred being sweeter than when you hurry after it too fast," she said. "Ki, I've never known a man like you before. Not that there've been all that many, but enough to know that you're different."

"That's a nice compliment, Darcy. Thank you."

"And I can still feel you in me. Does that mean there's more pleasure after we've rested a little while?"

"If you want more."

"You know I do. And Ki—" Darcy paused for a moment before she said, "I still want to learn more about *te*. But right now I think I'd rather learn just how much pleasure a man like you can give a woman in a single night."

Jessie felt the lugger's sail catch the wind and settle down to a steady course. Her eyes had long ago adjusted to night vision. She was lying on her side, facing the stern, just ahead of the single mast that was stepped in the center of the boat. She looked back toward the stern, where the two men who'd captured her were sitting.

They'd apparently left a bottle of liquor hidden in the sail locker, for one of them had his head thrown back, with the bottle tilted to his mouth. The other was still trimming sail, tugging at the halyard that ran through a block on the thwarts at one side. She could hear the creaking of the block

111

above the soft whistle of the wind.

Her position and the preoccupation of her abductors gave Jessie the first chance she'd had to see how much slack she'd been able to make in the thin rope that circled her wrists. Very carefully, she spread her forearms apart as best she could. The rope did not sink into her flesh, and she could wriggle her wrists a tiny bit inside the several turns of rope that circled them.

She applied a bit more pressure and felt the slack increase, but not enough to let her slip free. Gritting her teeth, Jessie spread her arms wider, until the biting of her bonds was too uncomfortable to endure. Then she relaxed for a moment and began to try to pull one hand free. The rope stubbornly refused to budge even the tiniest fraction of an inch.

"Hadn't you better stop swigging and see how the Starbuck dame's doing?" the man handling the lugger said.

Jessie froze and closed her eyes the instant she heard his voice.

"Hell, she's tied up tight enough. She ain't going no place anyhow, because there ain't no place for her to go," the second man replied.

"Yeah. I guess you're right. Well, pass me the bottle. We ain't got far to go, but we might as well enjoy the boat ride."

Counting on the darkness to hide her small movements, even as close to the men as she was, Jessie tested the rope again. It gave no more than before. The remark of the man who now held the bottle had reminded her that her time was sharply limited. Once she was in Dodds's hands, she'd be given no opportunity to escape.

For a moment Jessie lay motionless, thinking things through. She had little hope of freeing her hands in the short time that would pass before the lugger reached the north shore of the bay. Each minute that passed was important. She decided to risk the only other way she could think of to regain her liberty.

Moving very cautiously, keeping her eyes on the men in the stern, Jessie arched her back. During the voyage to Hawaii and back, she'd missed the regular exercise she got at the ranch, and her muscles protested as she stretched her arms downward. She pulled her knees up toward her chin, trusting the darkness and the preoccupation of her captors to hide her deliberate moves.

At first she did not think she could stretch her arms far enough or arch her back sharply enough to slide her bound wrists under her buttocks, but once she'd achieved that, the rest of her job was easy. She pulled and pushed until she'd gotten her bound wrists below her knees, then found that she had enough leverage to pass her feet one at a time through her arms above the binding on her wrists.

She lay quietly for a moment, her hands in front of her now. The men had not noticed her slow and cautious moves. Very carefully, Jessie shifted position until she lay on her back. By lifting her knees and twisting her hips sideways, she got her hands on the derringer in her garter holster.

Jessie lay quietly for a moment, debating with herself, but from the moment she got the derringer into her hands, she knew what she would be forced to do.

If her hands had been free, allowing her to aim and fire with her usual skill, Jessie told herself that she might have followed a different course of action. She had been in enough perilous situations to judge the most likely reactions of her abductors. They were not the kind of men who would raise their hands on demand and surrender to a woman, even if she held a two-shot derringer on them. They'd gamble that because she was a woman and her wrists were still tied, one or both of her shots would be wild. They might both jump her, or they might both go for their guns, but in one way or another they'd challenge her, and she'd be forced to shoot them.

Jessie's training and experience had taught her the dangers of wavering once she'd reached a decision. She rolled on her stomach, braced her elbows on the duckboards to offset the handicap of her bound wrists, and shot both men through the heart as fast as she could squeeze the derringer's double trigger.

Neither of them realized what had hit him. One fell back into the dancing waters of Fogarty Bay. The second slumped to one side and lay half in and half out of the lugger. Jessie let her derringer drop to the duckboards and crawled under the sail to the stern. She grasped the dead man's feet and lifted until his body followed the other man's into the bay. Then she sat down and worked at her bonds until she'd freed her hands.

While she worked, she reached a second decision, this one based on more complex reasoning than the life-or-death judgment she'd just made. Knowing nothing about handling a small boat, she was not totally confident that she could steer the lugger, and even if she'd been certain of her ability, leaving the small craft at the Baytown dock would be a giveaway. Much better, she decided, to let Dodds wonder.

She unwound the halyards from the cleat where they were secured and let the sail collapse at the base of the mast. Then, pausing only long enough to slip off her shoes and restore her derringer to its garter holster, Jessie slipped over the side into the icy water and began swimming ashore. Behind, a puzzle to whoever retrieved it, the empty lugger bobbed in the middle of the long narrow bay.

★

Chapter 11

Jessie didn't know how long she'd been in the water. Her body was numb, and the chilling effect seemed to numb her mind as well. The shore seemed almost as far away as when she'd slid over the side of the boat.

Her clothing dragged at her arms and legs and was growing heavier by the minute. She fought the temptation to discard it, for the chill had not made her brain too sluggish to think ahead. She knew that when she reached shore she'd need the protection of her skirt and blouse to cut the wind, for it was even colder than the water.

She began counting the strokes of her arms to keep her mind alert, to force her mind to concentrate on something other than the numbing cold. Twice she lost count and had to start again. Her arms grew heavier and heavier with each stroke, and she could no longer feel her feet.

Now and then something brushed against her thighs or legs and she forgot her growing exhaustion and flailed wildly in a sudden burst of panic at the unknown. Common sense quickly took control again, and she slowed her churning arms and legs to a steady stroking.

Ahead, the dark line of the shore, level with her eyes, did not seem to be any closer than when she'd started from the boat. She splashed on, resisting the temptation to stop and rest, for her mind told her that if she did, her clothing would drag her below the surface of the black water. She did stop twice, to let her feet sink, her toes searching for the bottom, but not finding it. When she tried the third time, she could not quite believe that the resistance her feet encountered was actually the bottom.

She let her weight rest on her feet and discovered that she did not sink. Still not quite believing, she brought her body erect and her shoulders broke the surface. For a moment she stood where she was, her breast heaving as she panted and enjoyed the luxury of letting her arms rest instead of flailing the water.

Lifting her heavy feet slowly and deliberately, Jessie waded to dry land. She stood for a moment, looking around. The night was moonless, and the darkness was complete except for a starglow which caused the bay and the land edging it to take on a faint luminousity. The wind sweeping off the Pacific Ocean and across the bay was even colder than the water had been, and she began walking to warm up.

Shivering almost constantly, Jessie made her way across the rocky strand. The starlight was bright enough to allow her to avoid the big boulders that were scattered along the graveled shore, but the gravel bruised her bare feet. Even at her slow pace, walking warmed her, though not enough to make her feel comfortable.

At last Jessie reached the Baytown dock. The lights that had shown in the larger vessels had been extinguished, but she had made up her mind while walking that she would not stop for help, but would go directly to the hotel. She turned away from the dock and started for the town. There were no lights showing in any of the houses she could see, but the dwellings did cut off the wind and she began to feel almost warm again.

Baytown's streets all converged on the path to the dock. She chose one at random and walked past the black windows of the sleeping houses until she could see the bulk of the two-story hotel ahead. The cross street she turned onto led past the dark windows of the *Gazette* office. Jessie walked by it and went around the corner to the street where the hotel stood, thinking that although only a few hours could have passed, it seemed a lifetime since she'd covered that same ground after bidding Ki and Darcy goodnight.

Light spilled out of the hotel doorway across the board sidewalk. Jessie reached the door and entered. Ki was bending over the desk clerk, who sat sprawled in one of the lobby's three chairs, a towel around his head. They did not see Jessie until she spoke.

"Is something wrong?" she asked calmly.

Ki whirled around. "Jessie! Where have you—" His mouth fell open when he saw her condition. Her blonde hair, still darkened by salt water, hung untidily down her shoulders, her clothes clung to her, her feet were bare and mud-stained. Then, as he did in moments when other men might have grown excited, Ki suddenly became calm. His voice normal, he said, "You've been in the bay, I see. Since your bed wasn't disturbed, but the door of your room was unlocked, they must have grabbed you as you came in. Then you got away."

"Your logic is faultless, Ki," Jessie replied, her voice as calm as his. "See if mine's as good. You came down to look for the clerk after you found my door unlocked. But he hasn't been able to tell you anything helpful yet."

"He was tied and gagged in the corridor to the dining room," Ki replied. "All he knows is that two men came in and knocked him out with a billy club."

"If he can look after himself, let's go upstairs where we can talk privately," Jessie suggested.

"I—I'm all right, Miss Starbuck," the clerk said. "I'm very sorry—"

"What happened wasn't your fault," Jessie assured him.

"But if you feel that you owe Ki a favor for finding and untying you, the best way you can return it is to say absolutely nothing about what happened this evening. And if you can get me some hot water, I'd like a bath as soon as possible."

"Why—well, if it will help you, Miss Starbuck, of course I'll keep quiet," the clerk promised. "And I'll bring up the hot water myself. There's a boiler in the kitchen."

"Good," Jessie replied. "Come on, Ki. We've quite a bit to talk about."

"I should have come back to the hotel with you," Ki said as they mounted the stairs. "This is something else that's my fault, Jessie."

"Nonsense. I knew Dodds was involved with the cartel, so I was a fool for being careless. But we won't be again." They reached Jessie's room; the door was cracked open, a streak of light coming from it. Jessie said, "I see my kidnappers were as careless here as they were on the boat. I remember now, they left the light burning when they carried me out."

"That's why I knocked," Ki explained. "The door was shut then, but I could see light around it. When you didn't answer, I tried the knob and found it was unlocked. I saw your purse on the floor and realized what must've happened, and—well, after that I went down and looked for the clerk."

Jessie led the way into her room, and closed the door and locked it. "I'll tell you what happened as quickly as I can, because I want to step into the bathtub as soon as the clerk gets it filled." Cutting all nonessential details out of her story, Jessie told Ki what had taken place. "And then I swam ashore," she concluded, "and walked back to the hotel."

"Not the most pleasant way to spend a substantial part of the night," Ki commented.

"No. I'm sure you were much more comfortable giving

Darcy some *te* lessons than I was outwitting the men who kidnapped me." Jessie smiled, then went as far as she and Ki ever did in speaking of the other's private life. "Darcy's a bright girl, Ki. She'll be better off for having known you. And we need her help and Eli's in handling our problem with Dodds."

"I had an idea that was what was in your mind when we finished talking to the two of them this evening. But surely you don't think Dodds is a member of the cartel yet?"

Jessie shook her head. "No. He's greedy and unscrupulous enough to be welcomed as a member in the future, but he'll have to serve an apprenticeship first."

"There's not much doubt the cartel's taken over his mill, or is about to," Ki said, frowning. "But I don't think he knows yet exactly what's happening to him."

"He doesn't now, but he will someday soon. And he'll have to be smashed, Ki. Not only for what he did to the Starbuck mill and for killing Tom Buck, but because of what he could do in the future. So, no matter how long it takes and no matter how much it costs, we'll stay here until he's finished."

Jessie, Ki, Eli, and Darcy were gathered in the parlor of Eli's house. They'd assembled in midafternoon, as soon as the delivery boys had started distributing the week's edition of the *Gazette*. The paper had been printed just as it had been set in type the day before Jessie's abduction. Darcy had wanted to tear the front page apart to get in a story about Jessie's having been kidnapped, but after listening to Jessie, Eli had overruled Darcy's plan.

"Jessie's right, Darcy," Eli had told his daughter gruffly. "I see what her reason is, even if you don't. Anyhow, you'll have a big enough story if we can get Dodds arrested for keeping coolies as slave labor in his mill, to say nothing of his bringing in that load of Chinese women for them."

Now, with the current week's newspaper off her mind, Darcy was renewing her efforts to get Jessie's agreement that the kidnapping incident be included in the bigger story she hoped to write if and when Dodds's plans were thwarted.

"But everything will be over by then, Jessie!" Darcy almost wailed after Jessie's latest refusal. "It wouldn't make any difference to our plans if I put it in a story then. And it would get my byline in the biggest papers in the country! The *New York World!* The *Philadelphia Bulletin!* The *Boston Globe!* The *San Francisco Chronicle!* Papers I've dreamed about!"

"That's exactly why I made you promise not to write a word about what happened to me last night," Jessie said. "And why I don't want my name or Ki's in the next story you write. I try to keep the Starbuck name out of the newspapers, Darcy, not get it in them."

"Before Darcy can be sure she'll get that story, there are a lot of things we'll have to decide," Ki pointed out. "And since we're not sure when the Japanese slave ship is going to get here, we'd better plan right now what we're going to do."

"I've already decided what I'd like to do," Darcy said. "I don't know whether everything would work out to make things happen at the right time, of course."

"Well, go ahead and tell us," Eli said. "It's your story, so you're the one who ought to say how you want to cover it."

"Just as long as your plans don't include anything that might keep us from capturing Dodds," Jessie stipulated quickly.

"If we don't capture Dodds, there's not much of a story," Darcy replied. "But here's what I'd like to do." She paused to gather her thoughts and went on, "I want to take pictures, and everybody's agreed they'll help in court. That means I've got to have daylight."

"Darcy, unless we've got a navy of our own, there's no way we can force that Japanese ship to come into Fogarty Bay and tie up at Dodds's mill in daylight!" Eli objected.

"I know that, Father," she replied. "But I can take some pictures of the ship coming into the bay, if my plan works out. And I think it will."

"Let's listen to Darcy, Eli," Jessie suggested. "I'd like to hear what she has in mind."

Darcy said promptly, "What I've got in mind is chartering Todd Kincaid's schooner. The *Santiem* can maneuver around outside the mouth of the bay, and the captain of the Japanese ship won't think anything's wrong, but all the time I'll be taking pictures. And I'll take pictures later of the Japanese boat in Dodds's dock, and maybe I can get the women to pose in the hold or wherever they had to travel. I hope they were chained together, or something like that!"

Eli shook his head. "You know the *Gazette* can't afford to spend as much money as it'd cost to charter Todd's boat, Darcy. But it's a good idea, all right, I give you credit for that."

"I'll pay whatever the schooner charter costs," Jessie said quietly. "I owe you that much, Darcy, for taking part of your big story away from you."

"And unless I'm needed somewhere else, I'll help you with your camera and equipment," Ki offered. "I know it's heavy."

"What we have is just the beginning of a plan," Jessie said crisply. "We need to go a lot further, though."

"I don't see how we can, Jessie," Eli frowned. "We might as well take it for granted that when the investigator from the attorney general's office gets here, he'll have some ideas."

"You're sure the attorney general will send a man, then?" Ki asked.

"Not as sure as I'd like to be. But we can't wait for a

federal marshal to get here from San Francisco or Seattle."

"We don't have much choice, then," Jessie pointed out. "If we don't go ahead and make our own plans, we won't have any plan at all. Darcy, the schooner is the key to your scheme. Let's go down to the dock right now and make sure we can get the boat. And we'd better be sure the captain knows what he's getting into and will work with us even if we get into a fight."

"We don't have to worry about Todd Kincaid, Jessie," Darcy said. "I know him well enough to be sure of that. He's a good captain, and the *Santiem* is a good ship."

In spite of her extensive travels, Jessie's mental picture of the captain of an oceangoing ship was that of most inland dwellers. She'd had a vague idea that the *Santiem*'s captain would be a brawny, craggy-faced man with a fringe of frowsy grayish whiskers and perhaps even a peg leg.

Todd Kincaid was a pleasant surprise. From his looks, he was still on the friendly side of forty. He stood as tall and lean and agile as a Texas Ranger, his firm jaw clean-shaven, his face deeply tanned. His manner was that of a man accustomed to command, concise and firm of speech, and bluntly outspoken.

It required little imagination on Jessie's part to see him in the saddle of a cow pony, galloping over the Western range, instead of ushering her and Darcy into the ship's low-ceilinged main cabin, and, with the smooth ease of any practiced host, seating them around a low table that bore the patina of careful and frequent polishing.

"All right, Darcy," Kincaid said when they were seated. "You say you're here on business, so let's get down to it. What kind of business is on your mind?"

"We want to charter your boat, Todd," Darcy said.

"Do you mind me asking why? I can't think of any reason the *Gazette* would need a ship."

"It's for the *Gazette,* Todd, but Jessie would be the one chartering your ship," Darcy explained.

Kincaid turned a pair of piercing blue eyes on Jessie. "Are you taking an interest in the newspaper, then, Miss Starbuck?"

Before Jessie could answer, Darcy spoke up. "We need the *Santiem* to cover what just might be the biggest news story that may ever break around here, Todd. It's—"

Jessie interrupted Darcy's eager spate of speech. "Don't you think we'd better ask Captain Kincaid to agree not to talk about our reason for needing a boat before we go any further?"

"You don't have to worry about me having a loose mouth, Miss Starbuck," Kincaid said. "I don't talk to anybody about the cargoes I carry or the ports I'm making for."

"Do you haul any lumber for Dodds's mill?" Jessie asked.

Kincaid looked at her, a frown forming on his lean face. "I don't see the point in that question, but I'll admit I'm confused right at the moment. What's the connection between you and the *Gazette* and Dodds?"

"There isn't any," Jessie replied. "Or rather, I suppose there is a connection, but it isn't what you might think."

Kincaid shook his head. "I don't quite know what to think right now. Your mill was Dodds's competitor before it burned, but you seem to be interested in his business. Are you working out some kind of deal with Dodds, Miss Starbuck? Because if you are, I'll save you a lot of time. I'm not interested in chartering to any business Dodds has a hand in."

"That relieves my mind a great deal, Captain Kincaid," Jessie said. "Now it's my turn to ask a question. Why aren't you interested in chartering to Dodds?"

"I don't make any secret of my reason," Kincaid replied promptly. "I chartered to Dodds some time ago to carry a cargo of lumber down the coast to Mazatlán. He paid half

123

the charter fee before I loaded; the other half was due when I got back and handed him a signed bill of lading. Dodds refused to pay what was due me until I'd signed for a second charter, picking up a cargo offshore and bringing it here. There was a catch to the new charter that I didn't like, and I refused it. I'm still waiting to collect the rest of my money from him."

"Do you mind telling me what the second cargo was?" Jessie asked.

"That was the catch. Dodds wouldn't tell me what I was expected to pick up offshore. I didn't like the smell of it."

Darcy broke in excitedly, "Jessie! Don't you think that second cargo might have been—"

"I'm quite sure it was, Darcy," Jessie broke in. "But I don't think we'd better talk about it just yet."

"I'd like to know what the hell—excuse me, ladies. I'd like to know what's happening here!" Kincaid said.

Jessie made up her mind. Kincaid's dislike for Dodds was obviously sincere, which would make him a valuable ally if he'd accept a risky charter.

"Darcy's been dying to tell you the whole story since we sat down, Captain," she said. "Suppose you listen to her, and then if you make up your mind to accept the charter, you and I can talk terms and conditions."

Darcy managed to condense her explanation to a three-minute narrative that covered the essential points. When she'd finished, Kincaid leaned back in his chair and stared at her and Jessie.

"If I understand correctly, four of you are planning to take on Dodds and his guards and the crew of a Japanese slave ship just to get a story for the *Gazette,*" he frowned. "Now it seems to me that's a pretty big order. Granted, you've got plenty of sand in your craws even to think about it, but—"

Jessie interrupted him. "You're overlooking one thing

we'll have behind us, Captain Kincaid. The law will be on our side. So will justice and common humanity, but I don't suppose they carry very much weight."

"Don't be too sure, Miss Starbuck," Kincaid replied. "I joined the U.S. Navy when I was still wet behind the ears to fight against slavery. As it turned out, I didn't get a chance to do much fighting, because I didn't happen to be on either of the two ships that fought sea battles against the Confederacy. But that hasn't changed my convictions any."

"Does that mean you'll take the charter?" Jessie asked.

"I'll make two conditions," Kincaid replied. "To be sure the *Santiem* is on the side of the law, I want to talk to the man you say the attorney general is sending. The second one is that if any fighting starts, you'll let me and my crew take a hand in it. If you agree to those conditions, you've got a ship."

★

Chapter 12

"Eli, if I hadn't known you such a long time, I wouldn't believe half of what you've just told me," Frank Bridges said. "I'd think you'd gotten me over here just to make a better story for that newspaper of yours."

"It's true enough, Frank," Eli told the Oregon attorney general's chief investigator. "It was just an accident that we learned about the women that are being brought in at the same time we got the truth about the coolies at Dodds's mill being slaves."

"Oh, I don't doubt your word," Bridges said. "Right after California passed their Exclusion Act, we had quite a few cases of ships trying to bring slave labor in through Oregon and Washington, but that's sort of tapered off since both states passed their own exclusion laws."

Jessie and Ki had been favorably impressed with Bridges from the start. He gave Jessie the impression of being much the same no-nonsense type of lawman as her friend Deputy U.S. Marshal Custis Long, a big man, tall and broad, with a sweeping mustache, a man who would at all times be in command of himself as well as of any situation that might confront him.

Bridges had arrived from Salem by horseback less than an hour earlier. His first act had been to get Eli Stone to call Darcy, Jessie, Ki, and Todd Kincaid together for a talk about their plans.

He'd agreed with Jessie that since such a long time had passed since the burning of the Starbuck mill and the death of Tom Buck, there'd be no point in trying to prove that Dodds had been implicated. When the talk moved to other aspects of the case, Bridges listened quietly. Finally, when Darcy explained her plan, he waited until she'd finished before offering his opinion.

"One thing bothers me about this scheme you've come up with, Darcy," he told the girl now. "That's the part where we cruise around offshore taking pictures before we get down to business."

"I told you why I want to do that," Darcy said. "And all of us agree that pictures of those women actually coming ashore—or just about to come ashore—would help when Dodds gets in front of a judge and jury."

"Well, I'd have to go along with that too," Bridges said. "And it'd be hard for a smart-aleck lawyer to say you took 'em for your newspaper instead of to help the case, because you can't use photographs in the *Gazette.*"

"Oh, I'll get some use out of the pictures," Darcy told him. "We can't print the actual photographs, of course. They're still trying to work out a way to make a printing plate from a photo print, but the engravers that will make the plates can use the shots I take as models."

"It's not that I object to pictures," Bridges frowned. "It goes a little past that. On seacoasts, U.S. jurisdiction starts at low-tide line and goes twelve miles out to sea. Suppose something happened and we had to intercept that Japanese slave ship to keep it from getting away. We'd be outside state jurisdiction, where I don't have any more authority than you do."

"Do you really believe that question will come up, Mr. Bridges?" Jessie asked. "Because if it does, a very good law firm in Washington represents the Starbuck interests, and I'm sure they could smooth over any difficulties of that kind."

"I'm just trying to look at things from every side, Miss Starbuck," Bridges replied. "I don't think there'd be trouble if I made an arrest in federal jurisdiction. And if there's any rough stuff, I can deputize Captain Kincaid's entire crew and make it legal for them to pitch in and give me a hand—always providing they will, Captain."

"Don't worry about my boys," Kincaid said. "They don't like slavers any better than I do. My men and I have another thing in common too. All of us enlisted in the federal navy during the War and trained to fight at sea, but none of us got a chance to fight. I know they'd enjoy helping."

"Well, that saves me asking a question I had for you," Bridges told Kincaid. "I don't mind admitting, I'll feel better about our chances if I don't have to take on the whole crew of that Japanese ship by myself."

"You know you can count on me for anything you need done, Mr. Bridges," Ki volunteered. "I have never done any fighting on the water, but I'll be there to do what I can."

"So will I, of course," Jessie said. "I hope you don't have any prejudices about women on your side, Mr. Bridges?"

"Not at all, Miss Starbuck. After all, if Darcy's going to be there taking pictures, I can't very well tell you that you'll have to stay on shore."

"Does that mean you won't object to meeting the slave ship outside the bay, so I can get my pictures?" Darcy asked eagerly.

"As long as we don't spook it off and keep it from coming in and docking in Fogarty Bay, I won't object," Bridges agreed.

"If it's not out of line for me to suggest something,"

Kincaid said, "I'd just about guarantee that if the Jap skipper tries to run away, I can maneuver the *Santiem* to herd that slave ship anywhere you want it to go."

"I'll keep that in mind, Captain," Bridges nodded.

"Listening to all that talk's got me mad at myself," Eli said. "Here's the biggest news story this town's likely to see in its entire life, and I'm tied down with a broken leg! I'm not even thinking about going along, because I'd just be getting in everybody's way."

"You've made a wise decision, Eli," Kincaid said. "You're right, it's better for all of us if a man in your condition stays ashore." He turned to Bridges. "It's almost noon now. Are we going to sail today, or wait until tomorrow?"

"I want to sail as soon as your ship's ready, Captain. We don't know when the slave ship will be here, except that it'll be soon, but we sure won't find it as long as we sit here in Eli's parlor and talk about it."

Kincaid stood up and said, "If there's nothing else, then I'll get on down to the dock and make sure the *Santiem*'s all shipshape. You can come aboard whenever you're ready."

"There's one more thing I want to say," Bridges told them. He looked at the others and said soberly, "Let's decide now what weapons we'll be carrying, and I'll tell you the conditions under which I'll expect you to use them. I hope we don't get into any kind of fight on this job, but if we do, I intend to win it!"

Jessie stood in the bow of the *Santiem*, watching the sun drop below the horizon. Below her, she was aware of the soft, sighing hiss of the ship's prow cutting through the blue-green water. They'd long ago passed through the surf line, where the regularly forming waves sent up froths of spray as they broke against the prow. Now the ocean's surface was a symmetrical maze of dimpled dots, darkening as the sun set. Except for a creak now and then as a stray puff of the brisk breeze put a strain on some part of the rigging, the noise of the water murmuring past the prow was the only sound that broke the stillness.

For the first hour as the *Santiem* pulled away from shore, there had been seagulls wheeling around, squawking raucously as they passed and turned and repassed the vessel. Now the gulls had winged back to shore. There had been sails in sight too, in the early afternoon, occasional patches of distant white, but now they too were gone. Each sail had brought a flurry of excitement, which faded to disappointment when the ships had kept their distance from the coast and continued north or south until the white patches dropped below the horizon.

To the west, the reddening sky was beginning now to define the line where the sea and shore met in an almost imperceptible arc. They'd been out nearly five hours, sailing back and forth in a series of long zigzags centered on the mouth of Fogarty Bay. Their course had never taken them out of sight of land, and at the moment the vessel was on a long tack that carried it away from the shore. Jessie looked back for a moment and found that she could no longer distinguish details on the rugged coastline. It showed now as a low black streak, the water between it and the ship a deep purple.

Ki and Darcy were standing on top of the cabin, with the heavy tripod that supported Darcy's camera between them. Darcy was making adjustments to the red leather bellows. The cabin rose at the center of the ship's deck and ended in front of the narrow poopdeck at the stern, where the steersman stood at the massive wheel. Watching him and glancing now and then at Ki and Darcy, Jessie did not see Todd Kincaid come out of the cabin and walk toward her. She gave a small start when she dropped her eyes from Ki and Darcy and saw him almost in front of her.

"Sorry if I startled you, Miss Starbuck," Kincaid said. "I just came up to tell you that I've arranged my cabin so that you and Darcy will have a place to sleep. There's not very much privacy on a vessel of this size, you know."

"That's very thoughtful, Captain Kincaid." Jessie looked at the captain's ruggedly handsome face and decided she was glad to have company after she'd been standing alone so long. She said, "And since we're going to be together in what seems to me to be very close quarters, I think formality is a waste of time. Please call me Jessie."

"Of course, if you'll stop being formal with me."

"That's what I had in mind," Jessie smiled. Then, suddenly serious, she asked, "What do you think will happen when we meet the slave ship, Todd?"

"That's a question I've been asking myself ever since I took your charter, Jessie. And I'm still asking."

"You do think we'll be able to intercept it, don't you?"

"If the slaver's heading for Fogarty Bay, I don't see how we can miss it."

"Even in the dark?"

"No captain in his right mind will sail into a strange port in the dark, Jessie. He'll hoist masthead lights and heave to a safe distance offshore. Then he'll go in after daylight."

"Is that what you'd do?"

"Of course. Especially in strange waters."

"You sound very positive, Todd."

"I am. There are reefs that stretch out for miles all along this part of the coast. They're charted, but unless the captain's sailed these waters before, he won't risk running his ship onto one of them. The bottom's very tricky hereabouts."

"I'd like to see your charts sometime, Todd. I'm a terrible landlubber. The only sailing I've done has been as a passenger on steamships. This is the first time I've been on a sailboat."

"Ship, Jessie," he corrected her. "A boat is rowed, and any vessel too big to be handled by twenty oarsmen is a ship. Would you like for me to show you around?"

"I'd enjoy it," Jessie replied as a sailor hurried up and began to pull at the knots in the doggings of the anchor.

"We're getting ready to heave to," Todd told her. "We'll lay offshore tonight right across the mouth of Fogarty Bay. I'm sure the slaver captain won't try to sneak past when he sees our masthead lights. Come along, Jessie. It's the mate's watch, so while he gets us anchored, I'll show you the *Santiem*."

"You lead the way, then. Where do we start?"

"From the hold and work up. And we'll just about be able to see all there is to see before supper."

On the forecastle, the gathering night had ended the experiments Darcy and Ki had been making with the camera. Watching Jessie and Todd talking, Darcy said to Ki, "It looks to me as though Jessie's going to take a lesson in sailing ships. Does the idea bother you, Ki?"

"No, certainly not. Why should it? Jessie has her own personal life and I have mine."

"Really? Why, I thought—"

"You thought wrongly, Darcy."

"She's very attractive, Ki."

"Yes. And a good companion."

"I don't have to worry about her being jealous, then?"

"Not at all. We walk together on the same path, but there is always a small distance between us. We both know it would not be good if we were to close that distance."

"If that's the case, since we can't do anything more with the camera until morning, do you think we might—"

"We will, if we can find a private place. Shall we go and look for one?"

During the next half hour, Ki and Darcy learned that the *Santiem* was much smaller than it looked from the dock or the deck. Wherever they went, they found sailors at work. Twice they encountered Jessie and Todd, and when they got back on deck, Frank Bridges was strolling between the cabin and the bow, puffing a cigar.

"Early to bed tonight," Bridges warned them. "The captain says his men will stand what he calls anchor watch, so we'll all have a full night's sleep and be in tiptop shape tomorrow."

Reluctantly, Ki and Darcy confined their parting gesture to a kiss and sought their bunks.

Bare feet pattering over the deck outside the cabin's portholes woke Ki before sunrise. He sat up in the makeshift bed that had been made for him on the cabin floor; beside him, Todd Kincaid and Frank Bridges were stirring in beds similar to his.

A sailor put his head in the cabin door and said, "Old Ben sighted sail, Cap'n. A barkentine making course this way. Might be the ship we're looking for."

"We'll up anchors and break out the sails, then," Todd said crisply. "I'll be on deck in a minute."

Ki reached the deck only a few minutes behind Todd. He scanned the horizon, but saw no sign of a ship. He followed the captain up to the poop deck. Two sailors were heaving at each of the capstans, fore and aft, while others of the twelve-man crew were climbing the rigging, getting ready to make sail. The steersman was already on the poopdeck, removing the lashings that had secured the wheel overnight. Bridges reached the top of the narrow stairs from the main deck and joined them.

Kincaid reached for the strap of the telescope that hung at the side of the binnacle and focused it on the western horizon. Gazing in the direction where Todd was pointing the brassbound telescope, Ki saw a muted smear of white against the light blue-gray of the predawn sky. He squinted at the smear, and after a few moments it took on the boxy outlines of square-rigged sails.

Lowering the telescope, Todd said, "She's still too far away for me to pick out her name."

He glanced at the *Santiem*'s rigging. The triangular foresail and mainsail were spread and beginning to fill, slatting only a little now as the men trimmed them to pick up the offshore wind. At the foremast, the outer jib was spread and the narrow flying jib was creeping up, the block creaking as the halyards grew taut. Slowly the schooner's bow swung toward the oncoming barkentine and began making way.

"We'll close fast in this morning wind," Todd said over his shoulder to Ki and Bridges. "Ten minutes, fifteen, and I ought to be able to pick up her name with the glass."

Ki noticed that Todd did not hurry any more than he wasted time. He gave the vessels ten minutes, perhaps another minute or two for good measure, then aimed the telescope at the barkentine again. He looked for several minutes, then took the glass away from his eye and shook his head.

"I can see the damn ship's name, but it's still too far to read," Todd said. He handed the telescope to Ki. "Here. You give it a try."

Ki got the glass focused at last and, after a moment, found that the trick in handling it was to move it very slowly to the point at which he wanted to look. He saw at once why Todd could not read the name. It was in Japanese ideographs.

"You couldn't make out the name because it's in Japanese," he told Todd. "It's called the *Asuka Maru*."

Bridges said, "There's not much chance of two Japanese ships being here at the same time, so this one's bound to be the slaver we're after. Todd, do you have any question about it?"

Kincaid shook his head. "No. It's heading toward Fogarty

Bay and it's got a Japanese name. That settles things, as far as I'm concerned."

"That's good enough for me too," Bridges said.

"Does the name mean anything, Ki?" Todd asked.

"No. There's an Asuka River in Japan; I suppose the owner named the ship for the river."

Darcy came running up the stairs to the poop deck. "Todd! Is that really the ship we're looking for?"

"It must be, Darcy. All three of us agree it is," he said.

"We'd better get the camera ready then, Ki." Darcy looked at Bridges and asked, "Or do you have something for Ki to do?"

"Not unless there's trouble," Bridges said. "Ki, go on and help Darcy get those pictures she's so set on taking."

"You said which side we'd go by first depended on the wind, Todd," Darcy reminded Kincaid. "Which side will it be?"

"With this quartering wind, we'll sail past her on our starboard side first. That's what you landlubbers call the right. We'll tack to port, and then tack again to put us on the other side of her. Isn't that what you wanted to do?"

"Yes." Darcy's voice was vibrant with excitement. "Come on, Ki! Let's get the camera set up and the plate holders ready!"

"You go on, Darcy," Ki told her. "I'll take a shortcut."

Bracing his hands on the poopdeck rail, Ki vaulted it, landing catlike on the top of the cabin. He had the tripod set up and was opening the camera case when Darcy came up the stairs at the bow.

"Showoff!" she taunted him laughingly. "I hope you'll move that fast if we have to find a new place for the camera."

"Don't worry," Ki said. "If you feel like it, I'll even climb the mast so you can get a picture from up there."

Darcy looked up from the plate holders she was stacking. "I wish this little ship of Todd's did have a crow's nest, but

135

there isn't one on either mast. If there was one, I'd be in it!"

Since the *Asuka Maru* had been sighted, the distance between the two vessels had sharply diminished. By the time Ki and Darcy had placed the camera on the tripod and Darcy had adjusted the bellows and set the shutter, less than a mile separated the schooner from the bigger barkentine. Darcy and Ki could now see the crewmen running back and forth on the deck, and as they drew still closer she gave a shrill, excited scream.

"Ki, look! Don't I see women in kimonos on deck now?"

Ki scrutinized the slaver closely. "Yes. A dozen of them, as near as I can tell." He did not take his eyes off the other ship, and after a moment he said, "There's a man among them too, Darcy, wearing a *hakama* and carrying a sword. A samurai!" he exclaimed in disbelief.

"Good. That'll make the pictures more interesting," Darcy replied matter-of-factly. "You'd better watch *me* now, instead of the other ship, Ki. I'm going to start shooting as soon as we get a little bit closer."

Very little distance now separated the two ships. Darcy put her head under the focusing cloth and began making the final settings while Ki stood beside the camera, holding a stack of plate holders. Darcy inserted a holder in the camera back and took out its dark slide.

As the distance between the *Santiem* and the *Asuka Maru* narrowed to a few hundred feet, she tripped the shutter and replaced the slide, handed the exposed plate holder to Ki, and grabbed another.

At the moment, Ki was more interested in the Japanese vessel than he was in Darcy's pictures. The schooner sat lower in the water than did the three-masted barkentine, and it was hard for Ki to see the deck of the bigger ship. He kept his eyes on the women lining the rail, and the samurai who seemed to be trying to get them back into the cabin.

The women were making a game of avoiding the man in flowing sleeves and wide, skirtlike trousers of dark blue. Ki observed that the man wore at his side both the traditional swords, the long curved *katana* and the shorter *wakazashi*. His hair was carefully dressed in the samurai fashion, shaved on top, the sides pulled tightly to the back of the head and bound there, then extending forward over the shaven top of the head in a narrow roll.

Only a few minutes lapsed before the *Santiem* swept beyond the *Asuka Maru* and began tacking around the stern of the Japanese vessel. The schooner completed its semicircular turn and started back toward the slaver. On the deck of the Japanese vessel the women began running to the port rail, the samurai all the while vainly trying to herd them into the cabin.

Several sailors began climbing the portside rigging as the *Santiem* raced toward the slave ship. Busy keeping Darcy's plate holders separated while still watching the decks of the slaver, Ki paid little attention to anything else on the other vessel until a shout rose from the main deck of the *Santiem*.

"Look out!" Frank Bridges called. "Todd, break out some guns! Those dirty bastards are getting ready to shoot!"

★
Chapter 13

Ki glanced up at the sailors climbing the rigging of the *Asuka Maru*, and saw that they had rifles slung across their backs. There were only a half-dozen of them, but even one or two riflemen shooting from above into the crowded deck of the *Santiem* presented a real threat. Aiming down, they could choose targets that otherwise would have been protected by the ship's gunwales rising above the deck.

"Come on!" Ki commanded, grabbing Darcy's hand. "We've got to get to cover!" Out of the corners of his eyes, Ki saw crewmen of the *Santiem* coming from the hold carrying rifles, and tugged at Darcy's wrist to start her moving.

"No!" she protested, pulling back. "My camera and plates, Ki! I've got to save them!"

"They won't do you any good if you're dead!" Ki snapped.

He lifted Darcy bodily and began carrying her to the stairs. A rifle slug raised a little fountain of water as it hit the ocean a few yards from the ship. Scattered shots were sounding from the deck of the *Santiem* now. Ki reached the main deck and started for the door of the cabin. Jessie was coming out as he reached it. She had a rifle in her hands, her Colt belted around her waist.

"Keep under cover in the cabin until the slaver gets

closer, Jessie!" Ki said. "Shooting at this range is just wasting your ammunition!"

"I'm a better rifle shot than most of those sailors, Ki," Jessie replied. "So are you. There's another rifle or two in there. Get one of them and come along!"

"As soon as I get Darcy inside." Ki carried Darcy into the cabin and let her down. She stood staring at him as though dazed. "Now stay here!" he commanded, hoping she'd obey him, but half certain that she wouldn't.

There were two rifles on the table, but no spare ammunition for either. Ki saw that one of the guns was a .45–75 Winchester; he checked the magazine, and when he saw it was full he did not even look at the other, but started for the door, carrying the rifle and levering a shell into the chamber as he ran.

As he started out the cabin door, Ki found his way blocked by the bodies of the crewmen outside pressing against the wall. An occasional flat thump of lead into stout oak told Ki the snipers in the rigging of the slaver were getting the range now. Todd Kincaid's voice sounded above his head; it took Ki a minute to realize Todd was standing on the roof of the cabin.

"Stay where you can't see the slaver for our sails!" Todd was shouting. "Remember, if you can't see them, they can't see to aim at you! Forget about shooting back right now!"

Ki glanced at the sails and saw they were no longer taut. He realized with a start that the *Santiem* was steadily losing way. Todd was running toward the wheel. He leaped up onto the poop deck and began talking to the steersman. The man turned the big spoked wheel, and the *Santiem* slowly responded. Her bow began to turn away from the Japanese ship.

A rifle barked above his head. Ki looked up. There were two sailors at the top of the foremast and two more halfway up the mainmast. They stood on the ratlines, the small tarred ropes that ran horizontally between the long shrouds that braced the mast. The thick mast shielded them, and they were aiming and firing through the gap between the mast and the gaff topsails. Then Ki realized that one of the two snipers on the mainmast was Jessie.

When he recognized her, Ki disregarded Todd's orders. Pushing his way through the crowd on deck, he made his way to the shrouds that slanted to the peak of the mainmast and clambered up the ratlines until his head was just below Jessie's feet.

There was room between the canvas and mast for him to slide the Winchester into the gap and aim. He picked one of the riflemen in the slave ship's shrouds and waited with his finger on the trigger until he could judge the effect of the mast's swaying roll on his aim. He squeezed the trigger and the big .45–75 slug with its flat trajectory caught the man in some vulnerable spot, for the sniper let his rifle fall and pitched from the mast into the rolling sea.

"Good shot!" Jessie said coolly. She looked down and saw Ki for the first time. "How did you get up here?"

"I was about to ask you the same question."

"I saw the sailors up here and it seemed to be a good place to shoot from, so I followed them up."

Jessie turned back to her rifle and Ki did the same. The reports from their guns came almost together, and two more of the few remaining snipers in the Japanese ship's rigging dropped.

There were only three men left in the *Asuka Maru*'s rigging now, and they began clambering down the ratlines as fast as they could scamper. Jessie and Ki fired another round, as did the men above them and those on the foremast, but shooting at a moving target from a rolling, pitching ship defeated all five of them. The three snipers on the slaver dropped the remaining distance to the deck and vanished behind the cabin.

Jessie's eyes had followed the snipers' descent and she gasped, "My God, Ki! They've got a cannon on that ship! Look!"

Ki looked just in time to see the gunner lay a torch on the touchhole of the brass cannon that was swivel-mounted in the *Asuka Maru*'s bow. Smoke belched from the cannon's mouth and the boom of the shot reached their ears just as the cannonball tore into the deck at the base of the *Santiem*'s foremast. The mast swayed and began to topple.

For a moment the rigging held the mast erect, then its base plunged through the torn deck and the mast toppled. The riflemen were tossed into the sea. The midsection of the mast crashed onto the ship's bulwarks and the sails it had supported settled in slow, ballooning puffs on the ocean's surface.

Ki glanced at the slaver. The gunner had turned the cannon on its swivel until its mouth was over the deck, and two sailors were reloading. Ki took quick aim and fired just as the *Santiem* responded to the drag of the mast and sail and the ship yawed and heeled and spoiled his shot.

Jessie had held her fire. She took advantage of the instant when the *Santiem* lay dead in the water in reaction to its yaw and picked off one of the gun's crew. The cannon had been reloaded by that time, though. The gunner had already swiveled it back and was aiming at the *Santiem*. He laid the torch on the touchhole an instant before the slugs from both Ki's and Jessie's rifles dropped him lifeless to the deck. Belatedly, the shots from the two riflemen in the rigging above them rang out. One of the men on the slaver's deck fell, but got up at once and began limping to the shelter of the cabin.

From the crowded deck below them, Ki heard Frank

Bridges shouting, "Lay flat on deck! Down, every—"

His voice stopped in the middle of the word as the cannonball tore through the bulwarks and plowed a lane of bloody death through the men of the *Santiem*'s crew who were standing in a compact group beside the cabin.

Neither Ki nor Jessie looked down at the deck below. They were trying to aim around the mast, but the fallen foremast and sail were dragging in the water, pulling the *Santiem* around, and the thick shaft of the mainmast now obstructed Ki and Jessie's view of the slaver. Jessie began climbing the ratlines to get higher, where the mast was smaller in diameter. Ki called to her, but she gave no indication of having heard him. He followed her up.

Again the *Asuka Maru*'s cannon boomed. The ball fell short and skipped across the surface of the water. It bounded from wave to wave, and though its force was diminished when it smashed into the oaken timbers of the *Santiem*'s side, the splintering noise that followed its impact told them that the ship's fabric had been breached for the first time.

"There's a new gunner handling the cannon!" Ki shouted to Jessie. "And more than likely another one standing by if we get this one! Give it up, Jessie! Let's get down before they shoot away this mast too!"

Jessie did not reply, but kept climbing. Ki followed. The diameter of the mast kept diminishing, and at last they reached a height at which they could get the deck of the slave ship in their sights. Jessie let off the first shot. Ki had not yet put his eye to the Winchester's sight, and he saw the slug from Jessie's rifle send up a spurt of water ten yards or more from the side of the *Asuka Maru*.

"Jessie!" he called urgently. "They're out of rifle range, but they can still reach us with the cannon! Let's get down while we've still got a chance! This mast is their target now!"

Jessie hesitated for a moment, then followed Ki as he

142

started down. When he reached the point where the shrouds were three strands wide instead of two, Ki stopped and waited for Jessie. She halted beside him.

"We're going to have to get off the *Santiem* before it sinks," she began. "We're still—"

Before she could finish, Todd Kincaid's voice rang out from the deck, ordering all hands to the boats. They looked down. Ki's eyes flicked across the confused scene on the deck, searching for Darcy, but her auburn hair was nowhere to be seen. Two of the surviving crewmembers were lowering the small boat that hung on the side of the ship farthest from the slaver, while two others were working at the davits across the stern, where a larger boat hung.

"Try to get in the big boat," Ki told Jessie. "More men on the oars means a better chance of getting away."

"All right," Jessie agreed. "But you get in it too."

"I will, as soon as I find Darcy. But let's hurry, or we might get left."

Jessie started climbing down the ratlines again. Ki waited long enough to take another look at the *Asuka Maru*. The gun crew had just finished reloading again, and now Ki saw the man in samurai garb standing beside the gun. He'd drawn his curved *katana*, and was waving it over his head in the style that only a skilled swordsman can manage, the blade of the sword revolving in his upraised hand so rapidly that it appeared to form a solid circle of shining steel.

Ki started down the ratlines again just as the gunner touched his torch to the cannon's touchhole. The big gun boomed as it fired, and Ki reached the deck seconds before the cannonball smashed through the *Santiem*'s bulwarks and plowed through the decking. The boards shattered as the cannonball tore a yard-wide path to the base of the main-mast.

Ki felt the mast begin to shiver with the impact of the cannonball, and dropped the last ten feet to the deck. He looked around for Jessie and saw her making her way to the stern, where the sailors in the longboat were motioning their fellows to hurry and get aboard so they could lower the boat.

Todd Kincaid was leaving the poop deck, heading for the longboat. Ki moved to follow him to the stern, but before he'd taken more than a step or two he got his first glimpse of Darcy since the uneven battle had begun. She was starting up the short flight of steps to the top of the cabin, where the red leather bellows of her camera was visible among a tangle of ropes and splintered boards.

"Darcy!" Ki shouted. "Darcy! Forget the camera! Come back! We've got to get off the ship."

Ki could not tell whether Darcy ignored his call or did not hear it above the hubbub of voices and the ominous creakings that were now coming from the swaying mainmast. The yard-thick base of the huge mast was grating ominously against the decking as it swayed back and forth. Ki could see that the iron collar that ran around the base of the mast and was fastened to the ship's deck with big bolts was beginning to pull away from the decking. He discarded his plan to hurry to the longboat, and ran after Darcy.

Darcy had reached the cabin roof by the time Ki started up the steps. She was on her knees beside the camera, paying no attention to the threatening noises that were now sounding at the base of the mainmast. The long red bellows and bulky box were half buried under chunks of wood blown from the bulwarks and the decking by the cannonballs, and Darcy was trying to uncover the camera to lift it.

As he got to the top of the steps, Ki could see past the rise of the poop deck. Todd was helping Jessie into the longboat, and seeing that she was safe, Ki hurried to where Darcy knelt. He took her by the arm and was lifting her to pick her up and carry her to the longboat when another

144

cannonball struck the *Santiem*. The big shot fell short of the deck, but struck the crippled ship on its side, just above the waterline. The ball smashed through the oak sheathing, already splintered by earlier shots, and hit the base of the mainmast.

Ki heard the crash and felt the ship shudder, and glanced up to see the mainmast swaying even more threateningly. He said urgently, "Darcy! Let go of the camera! We've got about ten seconds to get the last boat off this ship!"

"No, Ki!" Darcy wailed, her voice a mixture of anger and frustration. "I've worked too hard to get—"

She did not have a chance to finish. The strains and shocks already inflicted on the huge mainmast had weakened its supporting members too badly. The mast came crashing down. The big spar that formed the boom at the bottom of the mainsail swung wildly back and forth, inches above the top of the cabin, as the mast toppled. Ki saw the spar coming toward them just in time to pull Darcy to the cabin roof and drop beside her, sheltering her body with his own.

As the spar swung over them, Ki felt it graze his shoulder, then it was past, dangling by the metal eyebolts that attached it to the mast. Trailing ropes, snapped by the weight of the mast as it started down, fell across Ki and Darcy. The spar reached the limit of its arc and stopped with a snap that tore the eyebolts from the mast. The spar fell, pulling the mainsail down with it. The canvas billowed as it settled, a huge white bubble that covered the top of the cabin, trapping Ki and Darcy under its heavy folds.

"Ki!" Darcy called. "Ki? Where are you?"

Ki battled the enshrouding canvas folds to make space for him to raise his head. Darcy felt the pressure of his body against hers and began to stir as she recovered from her sudden panic. Ki pushed up the canvas so that they could rise to a crouch under the weight of the triple-thick sail.

"Are you all right, Darcy?" he asked.

"I—I guess so."

Darcy tried to sit up, but the weight of the sail was too much for her. She raised her head as high as possible, a few inches above the cabin roof, and tried to look around. The tentlike bubble of canvas covering them restricted their vision to the tiny space where they were half lying, half sitting.

Ki said, "Follow me, Darcy. I'm going to try to wiggle to the edge of the cabin."

He started pushing the canvas up with his shoulders just as another cannonball plowed into the ship's side.

In the longboat, Jessie looked back along the narrow space between the ship's bulwarks and the cabin wall, where she had last seen Ki. He was nowhere in sight. Jessie could not see the top of the cabin; it was hidden by the rise of the poopdeck. The sailors at the davits began lowering the longboat to the water.

"Todd!" Jessie said to Kincaid, "Ki didn't make it to the boat. He must still be in the ship!"

Todd stood up in the boat and looked back over the *Santiem*'s deck just as the mainmast toppled and dropped the sail over the top of the cabin. "I don't see him," he told Jessie. "And there's no way to stop the boat now."

"I'm sure he's on the ship!" Jessie said. "We were up on the mast, and Ki was right behind me when we got to the deck."

"What about Darcy?" Todd asked. "Did you see her anywhere on board?"

He stood on the seat and stretched his neck to make a final survey of the *Santiem* before the longboat dropped too low. All that he could see now was the canvas of the mainsail settling down in slow billows, covering the ship's deck.

"No." A sudden thought struck Jessie. She went on, "But Ki may have seen her and turned back to help her."

"He's probably all right," Todd assured Jessie. He did not mention that the mainsail might be covering them. "And I'm sure Darcy is too. We'll row around the *Santiem* after we get in the water. They can jump in and we'll pick them up."

Jessie settled back on the board seat. As the boat's keel touched the water, the cannon on the slaver boomed and another ball crashed into the crippled schooner. The small boat launched earlier from the port davits rounded the *Santiem*'s stern.

"Follow me," Todd called to the crewmen manning it. "We'll row along the starboard side."

"Hold on, Cap'n!" one of the men in the small boat called. "If we do that, we'll be sitting ducks for that damn cannon!"

"They can't hit small targets like we'll be," Todd replied. "And we've got to find Darcy and Ki. As far as anybody knows, they're still on the *Santiem*!"

Ki turned around, the rough canvas sail rasping across his shoulders. Kneeling now, he arched his back and began crawling toward the edge of the cabin roof.

"Keep close to me," he told Darcy. "Once we get out from under this sail, we'll be able to see what to do."

At the edge of the cabin, the canvas grew tight. Ki tried to heave up with his shoulders to lift it, but the task was too much even for his well-toned muscles. He tried to slip over the edge of the roof to get his feet on the deck, and discovered that the canvas was stretched too taughtly.

Reaching into the waistband of his trousers, Ki took out the short, double-edged knife he carried there, and began to saw at the tough sailcloth. The triple-thick fabric resisted his first efforts, then Ki managed to open a slit and the job went faster.

He sawed away until he'd lengthened the slit enough to

147

allow him to get through, then dropped to the deck and held the slit agape to let Darcy follow him.

They stood on the schooner's deck and looked around. The big canvas mainsail covered the rear half of the deck and was draped over the cabin. The fallen mainmast had crushed a big section of the bulwarks and was pulling the ship into a list. Forward of the mainmast, there were four bodies sprawled. Three were those of crewmen, the fourth was the corpse of Frank Bridges, half his chest torn away. Two big splinter-edged holes gaped in the bulwarks where cannonballs had torn through. The cabin hid both the stern of the *Santiem* and all of the *Asuka Maru,* and Ki cautiously peered around the edge.

Ki could not see either of the boats. Both were rounding the schooner's stern, out of sight. He turned his attention to the *Asuka Maru,* which was making way toward the *Santiem.* The barkentine's cannon was silent now that the schooner had been brought to its present helpless state. Many of the slave ship's crew were jammed into the prow, and among them Ki could see the man wearing the samurai robe.

"What do you see?" Darcy asked.

"That we'd better lower that small boat"—he indicated the boat that hung askew in its davits at the rail in front of them—"and get off this ship as fast as we can. The slaver's coming up for a close look."

"How can we get off?" Darcy asked. "That boat's smashed and the others are gone."

Ki looked more closely at the boat and saw that its prow had been wrecked by one of the cannonballs. He walked to the other edge of the cabin. The mainsail covered the deck there too, the long, heavy spar that had been its top boom slanting on the rail.

"Darcy!" Ki called. "Can you swim?"

"Of course. Why?"

She came up behind him. Ki pointed to the spar.

"That's better than a boat. It'll hold us up in the water and won't attract notice the way a boat would."

With his knife, Ki severed the ropes that connected the spar to the sail. The huge timber was fifteen feet long, tapering from a diameter of more than a foot to about eight inches. He tipped the spar over the rail and he and Darcy watched while it splashed into the water.

"Whenever you're ready," Ki said. He held out his hand.

Darcy looked at him, grimaced, and took his extended hand to help her to the rail. Ki levered himself up beside her. Hand in hand, they stepped off the rail and plunged into the ocean.

★

Chapter 14

"There's no sign of Ki and Darcy on the deck," Jessie said, craning her neck to look up as the longboat rounded the stern of the listing schooner and started along the starboard side. "Todd, don't you think one of us ought to go aboard and see if we can find out what happened to them?"

"I think we've got to." Todd pointed to the starboard lifeboat, dangling wrecked in its davits. "The boats we're in now are the only way they've got to leave the ship." Then, looking at the *Asuka Maru*, which was making way faster now, heading for the schooner, he added, "We've got just about enough time for me to go aboard and look before that Jap ship gets too close."

Todd swung the tiller, bringing the longboat alongside the schooner. The portside rowers shipped oars and when the boat nudged the *Santiem*'s hull, Todd grabbed one of the lines that had been a stay of a fallen mast and now trailed into the water. He yanked the line to test it and then hauled himself up, hand over hand, until he reached the deck.

Shouting their names at intervals, Todd walked around the cabin, but saw no sign of Ki and Darcy. He looked over the portside rail, but they were not in the water. He started toward the stern, but before he'd taken more than two or

150

three steps the cannon on the slaver boomed and Todd heard splintering of wood on the schooner's starboard side, followed by a ragged chorus of yells. He turned and ran around the cabin to the starboard rail, knowing what he was going to see, but dreading to look.

He stuck his head over the rail. The small boat had been splintered by the cannonball and was now barely awash. There were several men now swimming frantically toward the longboat. Todd counted quickly. Three more of his men were gone. He slid down into the longboat on the rope by which he'd climbed aboard.

"That damn slaver's close enough for us to be targets now," he told Jessie as he pushed the longboat away from the schooner. "I'm sorry, but I didn't find any sign of Ki or Darcy on board."

"Where could they be, then?"

"I don't know, Jessie. But we can't spend any more time looking. It may sound hardhearted, but we've got to save ourselves."

"Todd, I can't just go off and leave Ki and—" Jessie's protest was cut off by the boom of the slaver's cannon.

A fountain of spray rose a couple of feet behind the longboat as the cannonball crashed into the *Santiem* at the waterline. The longboat was amidships of the schooner; it could not turn to pull away from the slaver, which was bearing down on it at a fast clip. Todd chose the lesser of the two risks they faced. When the oarsmen dug into the water with their blades, he turned the tiller to head the boat directly toward the approaching ship.

"Todd!" Jessie cried. "What are you doing? We're trying to get farther away from that ship, not closer!"

"It's our best chance, Jessie," Todd explained. "He's got a better chance of hitting us if we're broadside to him than if we're heading at him. This way, all the target he's got

151

is the width of the boat, not its length."

"But what do we do when we get really close?"

"I haven't figured that out yet." Todd was busy with the tiller, swinging it from side to side, putting the longboat into a zigzag pattern as it drew closer to the Japanese vessel with each passing moment. "Give me a chance, though. I'll think of something."

Ki and Darcy hit the surface with a splash that stung their feet even through the soles of their shoes. Somehow they managed to keep their hands locked as they sank, and Ki began kicking with all his strength to bring them back to the surface. Their heads broke the water almost within arm's reach of the floating spar. A few quick kicks took them to it and they rested their arms on the floating wooden cylinder, letting it support them while they regained their breath.

They heard the crashing of the cannonball that smashed the small boat, and Ki said, "There must be a reason for the slaver to be shooting again. Let's go find out."

Ki began kicking with smooth, powerful strokes. He found that the spar went through the water as smoothly and buoyantly as a boat. Darcy joined him at once in kicking, and they moved swiftly around the stern of the schooner. They rounded the stern an instant after the second cannonball landed behind the longboat, and Ki called as loudly as he could, but the splashing of oars and the creaking of the oarlocks drowned his shouts.

"Todd's gone crazy!" Darcy said when she saw the longboat heading for the slaver.

"He's crazy like a fox," Ki replied. "He's made the boat a target that the cannon can't hit."

"But what's he going to do when they get right up to the slave ship?"

"I'll leave Todd to figure that out," Ki replied. "But if

we can move fast and get close enough to the slaver, maybe we can help him. Come on, Darcy. Let's kick!"

With the eyes of the slaver's crew on the longboat, and only their heads showing above water, Ki and Darcy escaped being seen as they approached the *Asuka Maru*. Similarly, those in the longboat were concentrating on watching the barkentine; they did not see Ki and Darcy. The spar and the longboat were on coverging courses, with the barkentine their common objective. All three elements of the triangle— the longboat, the spar, and the ship—were on a collision course, and the distance to the point where the three would meet diminished with each passing minute.

Jessie asked Todd, "Have you come up with any kind of plan yet? It seems to me we're getting dangerously close."

"We are. We're almost within rifle range now," Todd said.

Unexpectedly, one of the sailors at the oars spoke up. "If I can ship my oar, Cap'n, I'd like a crack at them slanty-eyed sonsabitches. I dropped a rifle in the boat here before we had to abandon ship."

"Let me handle the rifle, Todd," Jessie suggested.

Todd nodded and told the sailor, "Pass the gun back to the lady, Dave. She's the best shot in the boat. Besides, we need every man we've got on the oars."

"I hope you'll make good use of it, miss," Dave said as he passed the gun back. "I boughten it to shoot Rebs with, but the War ended afore I had a chance to use it. It's a good gun."

Jessie looked at the rifle. It was an old Henry, but in good condition and with a full magazine. She told Dave, "I'll do my best to make you proud of it, Dave."

Two snipers were already climbing the rigging of the

Asuka Maru. Jessie leveled the Henry and got one of the men in her sights. She waited for the longboat to stand poised on top of a swell and squeezed off the shot. The sniper plummeted from his perch into the sea. Without removing the rifle from her shoulder, Jessie covered the second sniper. Her first shot missed, but the second went home. The rifleman's body arced out and splashed into the water.

Jessie looked at Dave and nodded. "You're right. It is a good gun, Dave."

Now the crew of the cannon in the slaver's prow swarmed to service the gun. The gunner took his stance, his helper standing by with a smoking torch, ready to pass it on as soon as the gunner reached for it. Jessie brought the rifle up again. The bobbing longboat, zigzagging toward the barkentine, was proving to be a problem for the gunner. He adjusted his aim twice, then a third time, and extended a hand for the torch. Jessie dropped him before the flaming torch reached the touchhole.

Men swarmed over the cannon like ants. The samurai was striding back and forth behind the gun, his arms waving in angry gesticulations. Todd took advantage of the confusion. He set the longboat on a course straight for the barkentine and reached it without anyone on the deck noticing. He snuggled the longboat as close to the hull as possible without getting caught in the swell its sides raised in passing through the water, and signaled to the oarsmen to try to hold the craft there, amidships on the port side.

"Is this part of your plan?" Jessie asked.

"Not a bit. I saw a chance and took it," Todd replied. "They're sure to find us pretty soon, and I don't know what we'll do then. As a matter of fact, I don't know what we're doing now, except that they can't get at us with that cannon as long as we stay where we are."

• • •

Because they did not have to zigzag, but could push the spar toward the slaver in a straight line, Ki and Darcy reached the barkentine's starboard bow a few moments before the longboat pulled in close to the port side of the vessel. The sides of the ship loomed above them like an unscalable wall as they looked up.

"What are we going to do now that we're here?" Darcy asked.

"Find something to grab and hang on, if we can," Ki said, his eyes searching the side of the ship as it slid slowly past.

Not a rope, no projection or piece of ornamentation was visible on the moving vessel. The spar had drifted well beyond the midships point and the stern was in sight when Ki saw what he'd been hoping for.

"Be grateful for *sushi*," he told Darcy.

"What's that?"

"Raw fish, fresh from the sea. A Japanese addiction. Look."

Ki pointed to the stern. Four heavy trolling lines were stretched out from the railing, shifting lazily in the vessel's wake. Ki began kicking as hard as he could, and Darcy joined her efforts to his as soon as she realized what the trailing fishlines meant to them. The spar began to roll when it slid into the wake, but Ki put forth the extra effort he wasn't sure he had left to slide the end of the spar under one of the lines and grab it as the line slid along the heavy timber.

"Hang on to me!" Ki told Darcy.

She swam up to him and wrapped her arms around his chest. Ki let the spar go. The wake caught them in its boil and for a moment they twisted perilously, helpless to control themselves in the bubbling, foamy battle of crosscurrents. Ki managed to pull them along the heavy line. It was designed to hold big fish, but he knew there was a difference between the lunging of a hooked fish and the dead weight of two human bodies.

Gingerly, Ki pulled them ahead until he could reach up and grasp the rudder housing that protruded from the stern. After that, it was a matter of lifting Darcy up beside him, stretching to grab the splash-molding that extended several inches from the stern deck, and then they were standing precariously on the molding, their hands on the rail. A moment later, both had their feet planted firmly on the barkentine's deck.

A few feet in front of them, the steersman stood at the wheel on the poop deck, his back to them, facing forward. Past him, through the maze of rigging, Ki and Darcy could see the rest of the crew gathered on the foredeck, also facing forward, leaning over the rail, their attention riveted on the longboat containing Jessie, Todd Kincaid, and the remnants of the *Santiem*'s crew.

Motioning Darcy silently to remain where she was, Ki slipped up behind the steersman, who never knew what hit him as Ki applied an *atemi* hold to the man's carotid artery and he collapsed. Ki dragged the steersman's body back to the aft rail and heaved him over the side into the barkentine's roiling wake, then went back to the wheel and secured it with the lashings that lay on the deck next to it for that purpose. Ki figured that would keep the steersman's absence from being noticed too soon, since the ship would stay on a steady course for a while.

He beckoned to Darcy and then pointed toward the main cabin, which occupied the central section of the *Asuka Maru*'s deck. "In there, Darcy. We'll be out of sight, and as long as we're free, we've got a chance to get away."

There was a door in the aft wall of the cabin, and they ran for it. The door was unlocked. Ki opened it quickly and pushed Darcy inside. He closed the door and turned around to look at the interior, but his pupils had been so contracted

156

by the bright morning sun sparkling on the water that in the dim interior Ki found himself virtually blind.

"Can you see anything, Darcy?" he asked.

"No. Can you?"

"Not a thing. We'll have to wait until our eyes adjust."

A woman's voice came to them through the gloom. She spoke in Chinese. By her intonation, Ki took her words to be a question and replied in Japanese. A moment of silence followed.

"Maybeso you talk English?" the unseen woman asked.

"Yes." Ki's eyes were adjusting to the dimness now. He could see a pale moon of a face peering through a grille set in the door of what seemed to be a cell. He asked, "What is this place we're in? A prison?"

"So close is to be one," she replied. "You are who?"

"My name is Ki. She is Darcy."

"I am Lan Ling. You fight Moto's men?"

"Yes. Is Moto the captain of the ship?"

"No. Kiroshi captain. Moto boss over Kiroshi."

"Moto is a samurai?" Ki asked.

"Yiss. Is very mad, Moto, you kill guards."

Ki said, "Lan Ling, I know why you are here. You go to serve men of China who want women of their own land. True?"

"Yes. How you know this?"

"Never mind. I know there are other women with you."

"Ah, yes. Chun Yue, Ah San, Chie Ssu—"

"Never mind their names," Ki broke in. His eyes had adjusted to the dimness now. He could see Lan Ling clearly through the iron grille, and behind her he could make out the ten or so other women in the cell. The door, he noted, was locked with a simple sliding bolt, not a padlock. He asked, "Do all of you want to be free, to go back to China?"

"Oh, yes, pliss! But how?" one of them answered.

"Help us," Ki replied.

"How can help? Lock up."

"I'll let you out. But first you must tell me things I need to know. How many guards does Moto have?"

"Iss four now. You shoot others."

"And Kiroshi's men? The crew?"

"Iss twenty."

Ki was silent for a moment, then he said to Darcy, "There's no time for me to make any sort of plan, Darcy. You stay here with the women. I'll go back on deck and see what I can do to get us safely to shore."

"But Ki, I want to help!"

"I know you do. Right now you can help best by staying here where you'll be safe. Don't worry. I'll be back for you." He turned back to the grille. "Lan Ling, you and your friends stay here. Darcy will stay with you. If a guard comes in, crowd around her and hide her from them. Don't come on deck until I come back and tell you it's safe. Do you understand?"

Their vigorous nodding indicated that they did.

Ki slid the bolt to unlock the door, and opened it for Darcy to go into the cell with the women. He said, "I won't lock the door. One of you can stand and hold it shut if any of Moto's guards come in."

"Good luck, Ki," Darcy said.

She kissed him quickly, then went into the cell. Ki went out of the cabin, to face the crew of the slaver.

"I'm afraid they've seen us, Todd," Jessie said.

Todd had been scanning the side of the *Asuka Maru*, looking for a cargo port, or a Jacob's ladder left dangling, even a trailing rope—anything that would give them a way to board the slave ship. He followed Jessie's pointing finger. One of the sailors was standing at the rail, staring down at the longboat.

Jessie was still holding the rifle. She brought it up to her shoulder, but Todd pulled the barrel down before she could fire. The sailor's face disappeared and a moment later they heard him shouting.

"No use shooting," Todd said. "We're sitting ducks for them, Jessie. I've lost half my crew already. I'd just as soon not lose any more in a fight we can't hope to win."

Suddenly the rail above their heads was lined with men staring down at them. Two of the crewmen held rifles trained on the longboat. Todd raised his arms above his head and the others in the longboat slowly followed his example.

A Japanese wearing a cap, its visor outlined in gold braid, came up to the rail. The sailors parted to give him room.

"I am Kiroshi," the newcomer said, "captain of *Asuka Maru*. You give up to us, yes?"

"We're surrendering," Todd replied.

"You are captain of ship we destroy?" Kiroshi asked.

"Yes. Todd Kincaid, master of the *Santiem*."

"You will come aboard," Kiroshi ordered. "Bring no guns or other weapons, or you will be killed without mercy."

Kiroshi turned to the nearest sailor and gave an order. A moment later a Jacob's ladder was lowered over the side. Todd nodded to the crew. They pulled the longboat over to the slaver, and the sailor in the prow moored the boat to the ladder. Todd gestured for the crew to start up to the *Asuka Maru*'s deck.

With obvious reluctance, the sailor in the prow started to climb up. He was halfway to the rail when Moto pushed his way through the crowd of curious sailors on the slaver's deck and joined Kiroshi. The samurai's face was twisted angrily, his almond eyes mere slits in his broad, mustached face. The sailor on the ladder had stopped when Moto appeared, but now he continued to mount the Jacob's ladder.

He reached the level of the deck, his head and shoulders just above the rail. Without warning, Moto drew his long curved sword. Before anyone realized his intention, the samurai brought the blade around in a powerful side cut. The razor-sharp edge sliced through the sailor's neck as though it were butter.

The man's severed head fell in a long arc into the water. For a moment his dying reflexes caused his hands to grip the rail while a great spurt of blood jetted from his neck and rained down in a fine spray over those in the longboat. Then his grip relaxed and his headless body toppled into the sea.

★

Chapter 15

Ki sidled cautiously around the corner of the cabin just as Kiroshi was asking Todd if the remnant of the *Santiem*'s crew was surrendering. He listened to the brief conversation while he tried to plan his next move. It had been clear to Ki from the time he and Darcy boarded the slaver that *ninjutsu* was going to be called for, and the blazing mid-morning sunshine that now bathed the restricted area provided by the barkentine's bare deck would challenge the skill of even a professional *ninja*.

There was only one immediate possibility of evading capture, and Ki seized it quickly. He leaped up to grab the overhang of the cabin roof and swung himself up. Lying flat on the roof, Ki wormed to the forward edge. He arrived just in time to see Moto's brutal beheading of the *Santiem*'s crewman.

Ki watched Kiroshi grab Moto's arm as the samurai shook the sword once, smartly, to shake off the crewman's blood, and heard the captain say angrily in Japanese, "You dishonor your rank, Moto! The lowly sailor was harmless! He had no weapons!"

"These American dogs must be taught a lesson!" Moto retorted. "They have killed all but one of my fighters! They owe me five lives in exchange for those of my men!"

"We agreed that I will command as long as we are at

sea! You have pledged your honor as a samurai to this!" the captain said hotly. "I hold you to your pledge! Collect your blood-debt later! If we are attacked, you will command the fighting, but until we touch land there will be no more executions!"

"Very well," Moto replied sullenly. As he left the rail, he said to Kiroshi, "I wait, but I will collect my debt!"

Moto circled the cluster of sailors and went back to the rail, where he stood dividing his angry glares between Kiroshi and the occupants of the longboat. Kiroshi watched the samurai for a moment, then stepped up to the rail again.

In English, the captain said to Todd, "You and your men are safe, Captain Kincaid. I promise that Moto will not use his sword again. Come up on the deck, now!"

Kiroshi moved away from the head of the ladder to make room for the *Santiem*'s men to step down from the rail, and the crew of the barkentine crowded up in a semicircle to examine them at close range. As Ki had expected, the Japanese seamen turned their backs to the cabin. Poised on a corner of its roof, Ki waited for Jessie, and while he waited, he completed his plans.

One by one, the surviving sailors from the longboat came over the rail. Except for Todd, Jessie was the last to mount the ladder. When her head appeared above the rail, Ki rose to a crouch and signaled her.

Jessie's eyes widened involuntarily when she saw Ki, but she gave no other indication of her surprise. With a quick beckoning motion, Ki indicated that he wanted her to get as close as possible to the corner of the cabin. Nodding imperceptibly, Jessie stepped up to the rail and then to the deck.

Ki noticed that she did not wear her pistol belt, and wondered if she had left the weapon in the longboat, or had hidden it under her skirt. As she moved to the edge of the group of sailors, he saw the outline of the holstered Colt under her skirt and breathed more easily. Jessie ignored the curious stares of the Japanese seamen. She took her time moving to the edge of the group and turned to face the rail. Her position placed her less than a yard from where Ki lay.

Counting on the excited chattering of the *Asuka Maru*'s crew to cover his words, Ki pitched his voice low. He said, "I have a plan to escape, Jessie. In a minute, before they can lock up Todd and his men, I will challenge Moto and fight him. The crew will be watching us and you must slip away from them. There is a back door to the cabin, it is not guarded. Darcy is there with the Chinese women. Get them in one of the small boats near the stern and be ready to lower it to the water. Do you understand?"

Jessie bobbed her head a fraction of an inch. Casually, she took a half-step that separated her from the Japanese sailors nearest her. She was careful not to look behind her at the cabin, or to look up at Ki again.

Todd Kincaid came over the rail and stood facing Kiroshi. Ki was once more lying flat on the cabin roof, and Todd did not see him. Instead he faced Kiroshi and said, "I demand that the man who murdered my sailor be punished!"

"You demand nothing!" Kiroshi replied. "You will obey my commands now! Do you understand?"

Before Todd could reply, Ki jumped up. He spread his feet in the traditional Japanese fighting stance and called loudly, "Kiroshi! *Katajikenai!*"

Having delivered the cutting insult that in his own language meant Kiroshi had suffered great loss of stature, Ki switched to English, to prepare Todd and his men for what he planned to do.

"You have allowed a man under your protection to be murdered by one who calls himself a samurai!" Ki did not know how much English Moto understood, and framed his next words to infuriate the killer. Still facing Kiroshi, he

163

went on, "You have been shamed and you have not washed your shame away with blood! I will do that for you, Kiroshi! I will fight the *yakuza!*"

When Moto heard himself described as a *yakuza,* a mere gangster not entitled to wear the long sword of honor, but only the short sword allowed to commoners, he started from the rail with a roar of rage, drawing his *katana* from his sash.

Still speaking Japanese, Ki taunted him, "Put down the sword of honor, *yakuza!* Are you so stupid that you don't know the Emperor forbade the wearing of the *katana* more than a dozen years ago, or do you choose not to obey the command of the Son of Heaven?"

Moto's back stiffened at Ki's reproof, and he replied, "The Emperor's edict is law only within the Empire. Those samurai who wish to dishonor their ancestors by giving up the long sword and becoming shopkeepers and farmers may do so. Those who wish to commit *seppuku* rather than obey may do so. For my part, I prefer to see that the way of the samurai is not forever lost, even though I must disobey my Emperor and live in exile in China and on the high seas. As for you, you have no sword at all! Who are you to challenge a samurai?"

Ki spoke one word. It was a word that seldom passed his lips, the family name borne by his mother. Moto lowered his *katana* and stared at Ki. Then he nodded slowly.

"I will fight you," he announced. "But you have no sword."

As Ki had anticipated would be the case, his challenge and the exchange between himself and Moto had frozen Kiroshi and the crew in their places. No one had moved when he shouted his challenge, nor had anyone noticed Jessie's quiet departure when the exchange of insults was at its peak.

Ki jumped from the cabin and landed catlike on his feet

in the narrow space between the cabin and the rail. He reached for the weapon he'd chosen when he planned his challenge: a belaying pin from the half-dozen that rested in their slots just below the rail. He held up the hardwood pin, more than two feet long and over an inch in diameter.

"This will serve," he told Moto, holding up the pin. "I need no *katana* to defeat a *yakuza*."

Moto's anger and outraged pride drove him to say what Ki had been sure he would. The samurai laid his long curved sword on the deck and drew the shorter *wakazashi* from his sash.

"To prove my samurai honor," he said curtly, "we will meet on even terms."

With a half-bow, little more than a nod, Ki acknowledged Moto's statement. He took a step toward the samurai. Moto brought up the short sword to parry the expected attack, but Ki did not raise his weapon as he made a quick advance. He brought the pin in low, the tip aimed at Moto's feet. Moto dropped his arm to parry and Ki twirled the pin, striking Moto's wrist. The blow was a hard one. The tip of the pin caught the long tendon at the base of the samurai's thumb. Moto's hand flew open and the short sword clattered to the deck.

Instead of pressing his attack, Ki smiled mockingly and stepped back to allow Moto to pick up the *wakazashi*. The gesture of courtesy fed Moto's anger. He snatched the sword from the deck and, as he raised it, lunged with an upward thrust at Ki's abdomen. Ki tapped the blade aside, and as Moto's lunge brought him close, Ki brought the pin up on the inside of his adversary's elbow. The pin struck the median nerve at its most vulnerable spot. Moto's arm quivered uncontrollably. He dropped the *wakazashi* a second time.

A few snickers sounded from the crew as Ki stepped back to let Moto pick up the sword again.

The samurai picked up the short sword with his left hand and was working the fingers of his right to restore their feeling. Ki shifted the belaying pin to his left hand. The attack of a left-handed swordsman, whose every move is opposite to that of a right-handed opponent, can confuse even an expert and cause him to make serious and often fatal mistakes. Moto drew down the corners of his mouth as Ki switched hands with the belaying pin. Ki replied to the samurai's sour grimace with a bland smile.

Moto advanced more cautiously when he began his next attack. He held the *wakazashi* in front of his chest, its point tilted upward, directed at Ki's throat. Ki was ready to finish the fight. He took a step to one side. Moto shifted his feet to maintain the threat of the sword's sharp point.

Ki feinted forward, and when Moto thrust with the sword, Ki once more swung his torso aside. He made a feint of his own, a fast thrust at the *wakazashi* with the pin's tip. Moto let the pin rasp against the blade, then twisted his wrist sharply downward. The parry turned the tip of the belaying pin aside while Moto's blade passed under the *it* and darted for Ki's chest.

Ki sidestepped. Like his previous move, this one took him in the semicircular path he'd plotted to carry him to the prow. The spectators turned with him. Moto pressed his attack with a vicious sweep of the *wakazashi*.

Ki retreated still farther, pulling the watching sailors with him. The last step of his retreat swung Moto far enough around to place the cabin at his back as well as at the backs of the *Asuka Maru*'s crew. When Moto lunged again, Ki dropped the tip of the belaying pin to stop the sword's sweeping blade, but still stepped backward as the deflected blade passed his legs.

Moto was both angered and encouraged as Ki continued to retreat. He attacked more boldly now, with an overhead cut that Ki parried. As the sword blade slid off the belaying pin, Moto converted its downward path to a sideways slash that came so near Ki's legs that the blade's tip cut through a fold of his trouser leg as Ki stepped back.

Ki's tactic of retreating instead of parrying to avoid Moto's slashing tactics had brought him to his objective now. He was no more than a long stride away from the brass cannon, where the bucket of live coals that kept the firing-torch alight still smoldered. He did not risk looking away from Moto's sword to check the gun's location, but knew that he was close enough to his goal to bring the fight to a climax.

Moto had gained confidence each time Ki retreated, and was pressing hard now. His *wakazashi* was constantly in motion, its tip darting forward like the head of a striking snake, but always Ki's parry turned it aside at the last split second. The samurai quickly switched the sword to his right hand, and with the fresh strength gained from the rest its muscles had enjoyed, Moto closed in, slashing with quick wrist-twists that set the tip of the blade dancing in a figure-eight before Ki's eyes.

As Moto took a half-step forward, Ki held his ground. His eyes were watching the shining sword tip, waiting for the tiny deviation of the pattern it described that would give him warning of the point Moto planned to attack. The deviation came, an almost invisible break, which Ki caught just in time. Moto's wrist stiffened and he lunged. Ki had shifted his hand to the center of the pin and was ready. When Moto lunged and the blade darted for Ki's throat, Ki swept it aside with a ringing clash.

His blow was hard enough to send Moto's arm swinging back. Ki grasped the pin with both hands and drove one end into Moto's belly with all the strength he could muster, and as the pin met elastic flesh and muscle, it rebounded. Ki used the impetus of the rebound. Twisting the pin, he sent the top end crashing into Moto's larynx.

167

Tissue tore and cartilage crackled as the tip tore into Moto's throat. The samurai was already breathless from the smash into his abdomen. His arms drooped in spite of his efforts to raise them. The *wakazashi* dropped from fingers suddenly nerveless. Moto's mouth gaped and a strangled whistling came from his shattered throat. He sagged slowly to the deck, his body writhing as he strangled on his own blood.

Ki dropped the belaying pin while Moto was still crumpling; the eyes of the sailors were all fixed on the samurai's sagging form. He took the long stride needed to reach the bucket of coals and, grabbing its bail, circled the stunned huddle of sailors, strewing the deck with red embers as he ran toward the door in the forward end of the cabin, from which he'd seen the powder-bearers emerge earlier. Opening the door, Ki tossed in the bucket, still a third full of glowing coals.

"Todd!" Ki shouted as he ran toward the stern. "Get off the ship, quick! Dive! Get your crew in the longboat and row fast!"

Looking over his shoulder as he raced for the stern, Ki saw the men of the *Santiem* fighting their way to the rail. He got to the boat where Jessie and Darcy waited with the Chinese women.

"Let's get the boat in the water in a hurry!" he said. "We don't have time to waste!"

"Push us over the rail and get in, then," Jessie told him. "I thought we'd have to leave fast, so Darcy and I have figured out how these pulleys work. And Lan Ling's been telling her friends how to row."

Ki shoved the side of the boat. The davits squeaked as they turned, but swiveled in their sockets until the boat was held in midair outside the rail, dangling over the water. Ki leaped aboard, and several of the women began paying out the ropes that lowered the boat to the water. Ki looked toward the barkentine's bow and saw the heads of Todd and his crew breaking the water as they swam for the longboat.

Jessie and Darcy released the swivels of the fallblocks and Ki gave the boat a mighty shove to get it as far from the slaver's side as possible. Lan Ling chattered out a command and the women picked up the oars that had rested on the seats beside them and fitted them into the oarlocks. They rowed raggedly and slowly, but the boat started moving away from the ship.

"What did you do?" Jessie asked. "Toss a match in the powder magazine?"

"I didn't have a match," Ki replied. "So I threw in the bucket of live coals they used at the cannon. It's taking a long time, though. Maybe the coals didn't get to the magazine after all. But there were enough to start a good fire, anyhow."

At that moment the *Asuka Maru* exploded. The main deck rose into the air, carrying the cabin with it, breaking up as it rose, and the air was suddenly filled with debris dropping from a huge cloud of smoke. As the air cleared, they saw the sides of the barkentine bulge out and crack and the bow and stern dip below the surface. Around the broken ship, the ocean heaved and rolled.

A few moments later the shock wave from the explosion reached their boat. The little craft rocked furiously, shipped water, and was almost swamped as it tossed on a series of big waves. The Chinese women held on to the sides and the seats and screamed as the boat tossed. Ki held on too, while he watched the two halves of the broken barkentine raise themselves almost to a vertical position and then disappear below the surface.

Darcy broke the silence that followed the blast. She pointed and said, "Todd and some of his men made it to the longboat. And look! The *Santiem*'s still floating!"

Ahead of them, the longboat with its sadly diminished

crew was swinging toward the *Santiem*. The shock wave of the explosion was just reaching the schooner, and it rose and fell as the ocean heaved, but gave no indication that it might sink. Todd waved and pointed to his vessel. Ki stood up and replied with a wave.

"Tell your friends to start rowing again, Lan Ling," he said. Sitting down, he took the tiller and steered in the wake of the longboat until they reached the listing schooner's side.

"It's hard to kill a good ship," Todd said when they pulled in beside the longboat, moored nose-in to the *Santiem*'s battered hull. "I think she'll sail again one of these days."

"I'll pay whatever it costs to fix your ship, Todd," Jessie said quickly. "If you hadn't chartered it to me, it wouldn't be in the shape it is now. And I'll see that the families of the men you lost are taken care of, too."

"Well—" Todd began.

"No wells or buts," Jessie said firmly. "I mean what I say and I won't listen to your arguments."

"I wasn't going to argue, Jessie. I was just trying to think of a way to say thanks," Todd replied.

"I'm not doing it for thanks, Todd, but because it's the least I can do for all the trouble I've stirred up here."

"Seems to me you've still got a little bit to stir up," Todd said quietly.

"Yes," Darcy put in. "Trouble by the name of Dodds."

"Ki and I will handle him in our own way, Darcy."

"Hold on, Jessie!" Todd exclaimed. "All that trouble you said a minute ago you'd given me was really caused by Dodds. And don't forget, I've got some unfinished business of my own to settle with him. So don't deal me out until it's finished."

"But your ship—" Jessie began.

Todd held up a hand to stop her. "I'll leave a couple of

my men here, just so nobody can claim her for salvage, then I'll go right along with you."

"And in case you'd planned on my quitting, Jessie, I'm not about to, any more than Todd is," Darcy said firmly.

"If we've all had our say, then, we'd better start for shore," Ki suggested. He looked at the sun, midway to the western horizon. "If we start now, we should just about make it to Fogarty Bay before dark."

Lan Ling and the other Chinese women had been listening to their conversation. Now Lan Ling asked, "You take us with you, pliss?"

"Of course we will!" Jessie replied. "We didn't get you off that slave ship just to leave you stranded here."

Rowing to shore took less time than they'd thought it would, with the offshore wind at their backs. The sun was still well above the horizon's rim when Todd pointed out the little gap in the shoreline that marked the mouth of the bay. The distance between boat and shore narrowed rapidly, and soon they were able to see the buildings of Dodds's mill above the high fence that surrounded it.

"If we had any guns and a few more men, I'd be tempted to stop and take care of Dodds on the way in," Todd said.

"It's not the time," Jessie said. "Don't worry, Todd. We can wait another day."

Todd had just turned the tiller to set the boat on a long sweep that would take them to the mouth of the bay when a file of men carrying rifles emerged from the mill gates and began forming a line along the point.

Todd shouted to the women to stop rowing. "It looks like we're going to have to land somewhere else," he said grimly. "It'd be suicide to try to go through that narrow gap. Dodds's men could kill all of us with a single volley, and there wouldn't be a thing in the world we could do to stop them!"

★

Chapter 16

Jessie looked along the shore. As far as she could see to both the north and south, the waves were dashing high and white against stone cliffs whose towering faces rose sheer from the water, or roiling between massive boulders that broke the surface as far as a mile or more from land.

"It looks awfully rough and rocky," she said. "Are there places to the south where we can go ashore safely?"

"Not many, but a few," Todd replied. "And we're ten or twelve miles from the nearest." He looked at the sun, now dropping to the western rim of the ocean. "We'll have to row fast."

For more than an hour, taking turns at the oars, they rowed south, paralleling the rugged coast. Their progress was painfully slow, but at last Todd steered for the shore. They bounced into a cleft that broke the ribbed stone face of a towering headland and slid into the calm water of a pocket-sized bay. A sandy beach not much wider than the boat lay at the water's edge. The prow grated on the sand and the rowers laid their oars aside with sighs of relief.

"We've made it this far," Todd told them. "Now we've only got another mile or so to go and we'll be in a sheltered place where there's a freshwater spring."

"Fresh water? And something to eat, I hope?" Ki asked.

"Good water, yes. There might be a few berries," Todd

replied. "We'll have to pull in our belts tonight."

"You mean we can't get to Baytown until tomorrow?" Jessie asked.

"We'd be fools to try," Todd told her. "It's getting late, and I've only been over the trail twice. I might miss it in the dark. Besides, most of it's over real rough ground."

"I'm less worried about rough ground than I am about Dodds and his gang of gunmen following us here," Ki said. "We never did get out of sight of land today. Dodds must know what happened, or he wouldn't have been waiting to meet us."

"We'll stand watch tonight," Todd said thoughtfully. "And take our chances on getting through tomorrow."

"If we've still got a mile to go, we'd better get started," Jessie observed. "I'd hate to shepherd these women over a rough trail in the dark."

For the first quarter-mile after leaving the boat, they made slow work of climbing up a narrow ravine. When the ground grew level, the party stumbled for another half-mile over cracked and broken rock. Suddenly the barren stretch ended, and they passed between tall firs and round ground-hugging cedars that grew in thin soil covered with prickly knee-high vines.

They did not need to be told when they reached the spring. It rose in a small, sparsely grassed clearing, forming a clear, rippling pool. They stopped to look at the water for only a moment before rushing as one to drop to the ground at the edge of the pool and burying their faces in the sweet bubbling liquid.

"Oh, this is wonderful!" Jessie exclaimed, lifting her face from the pool, drops of water beading over her cheekbones and running down to drip off her chin. "So many things have been happening so fast that I didn't realize how thirsty I was!"

"I don't think any of us did," Ki said. He looked around

the shaded pond, where the Chinese women and the seamen from the schooner were still drinking from cupped hands and splashing cold sweet water on their faces. He gazed up through the branches of the tall pines at the sky and added, "I don't think we realized how soon it's going to be dark, either. We'd better fix up some kind of camp, if we're staying here tonight."

"We break branches off trees," Lan Ling volunteered. "Make plenty soft beds."

"What about Dodds?" Darcy asked. "Todd, do you think he knows about this place?"

"If he's ever been south of Fogarty Bay, he does," Todd replied. "Anybody who's ever taken the coast trail knows it's the only sweet water for ten miles in either direction."

"If Dodds was ready to stop us at the mouth of the bay, he certainly won't let ten or fifteen miles keep him from trying to stop us now," Jessie said thoughtfully. "How long would it take him to get here, Todd?"

"If he started when we did, he wouldn't be too far behind us. Three hours, maybe four."

"Don't you think he'd wait until morning?" Darcy asked. "He could set up an ambush on the trail easily enough."

"I don't think we can risk trying to second-guess him," Jessie said. "We need to put a lookout on the trail from the north tonight, in case he attacks us here at the spring."

"We'd better guard the longboat too," Todd suggested. He turned to the seamen. "Dave, you and Sam and Grant handle that."

Ki asked, "Todd, is there a good place along the trail to watch for Dodds?"

"Yes. About a mile from here the trail runs across a half-mile stretch of bare rock he'd have to cross."

"Then that's where our sentry ought to be," Jessie said. "Suppose you and I go up and stand watch?"

"I'm ready if you are, Jessie. But I wish we had a gun."

"We have," Jessie said. Turning her back, she reached up under her skirts and brought out the Colt. "And I'm as ready as I'll ever be, so let's go while it's still daylight."

Except for the faint trail, almost invisible in places, they might have been walking over unexplored ground after they'd gotten a few hundred feet from the spring. As they went farther, the trees grew closer together, and the undergrowth thicker.

"Wait a minute!" Todd said as they entered a small glade. "That looks like a patch of berries over there."

"Let's go look. I'm hungry enough to eat anything."

They walked over to the tangle of waist-high vines, and even before they'd gotten close, Jessie could see the blue-purple huckleberries glistening among green leaves. She ran to the edge of the patch and began picking. The berries were full of seeds, but their tart sweetness satisfied her hunger, of which she hadn't really been aware until now.

Todd was picking and eating a few paces away, and Jessie had turned to speak to him while she stepped farther into the patch. Suddenly the vines in front of her heaved and rustled. She turned, her hand reaching for her Colt, then froze with sudden shocked surprise when, out of the vines, a black bear a foot taller than she was reared up in front of her. Its red mouth, rimmed with yellow teeth stained with berry juice, yawned in her face. The bear rumbled angrily and Jessie brought up her Colt, but Todd's shout froze her finger on the trigger.

"Don't shoot him!" he warned.

Todd started at a run toward the bear, waving his arms and shouting gibberish at the top of his voice. The bear whuffed and instinctively Jessie raised her Colt, but before she could fire, the animal dropped on all fours and ran for the trees. The bear was out of sight at once, and Jessie was still standing frozen in place, when Todd came up to her.

"Are you all right?" he asked, putting an arm around her waist.

At the friendly touch, Jessie began trembling in reaction from the shock. Todd folded his arms around her and held her close to him while she shook out of control for a few seconds. At last the reaction subsided and she found her voice.

"I'm fine," she said. "And I feel like a fool. It's not that I was scared as much as I was surprised."

"Bears make you feel that way," Todd told her. "But I'm glad you didn't shoot him. A pistol's no gun to shoot a bear with, Jessie, not even at close range. He'd have turned mean if you'd wounded him, and maybe torn us both up."

Jessie said nothing. She's realized that for the first time in many weeks she was in a man's arms, being held by muscular arms and pressing against a hard firm body. She made no effort to free herself, and after a moment Todd gave an embarrassed cough and released her.

"I didn't mean to grab you up that way," he said. "I hope you're not mad at me."

"I'm not a bit mad, Todd." Jessie paused and decided to say what was in her mind. "In fact, it felt good to have a man holding me."

"Well," Todd said, "we've still got a little ways to go, and I guess I had my fill of berries. Maybe we'd better get on."

They walked on in silence the short distance to the rocky stretch that Todd remembered. His recollection had been correct. The ground for a space of more than a quarter-mile was barren of vegetation where the solid rock surfaced. Twilight was ending fast and the approaching night brought a chill to the air.

"Over there, I think," Todd said, pointing to a thick clump of baby cedars. "The trees will break the wind. We

176

can stretch out and be comfortable while we keep a lookout."

Lying side by side but still carefully apart in the cedar grove as the twilight faded, Jessie and Todd were silent until the wet, chilling wind that had come up with dusk started Jessie to shivering.

"This cold, raw air goes through you," he said. "I don't guess you're used to it, are you?"

"No. I spend as much time as I can on the Circle Star, in West Texas, where the air's thin. Unless there's a wind, it doesn't cut into you like this does."

"We can't build a fire, but if you're cold, we can huddle up together," he suggested a bit hesitantly.

"That would be nice. I am getting chilled."

They rolled together and Jessie snuggled up to Todd. He put his arms around her and held her close to him. Soon she began to grow warm. She shifted her position and the change brought Todd's weight on her. Her face was turned to him, her head resting on his shoulder, and when Todd exhaled, the warmth of his breath caressed her ear and neck. The pressure of Todd's firm chest on her breasts had brought her nipples erect, and when one or the other of them moved, the small scraping of her camisole sent a tingle through Jessie.

She stirred restlessly, and Todd asked her, his voice husky in the dark, "Does it bother you when I move?"

"No. At least not the way you meant it."

"You're not thinking the same thing I am, are you?"

"I imagine I am, Todd. It'd be impossible not to, lying here the way we are."

Todd moved his head and, in moving, scraped his chin against Jessie's neck. Her body twitched involuntarily at the rasping of his stubbled chin against the sensitive area.

Surprise and pleasure mingling in his voice, he whispered, "You are thinking what I am."

Jessie discarded pretense. She slid her hand between their

bodies, found Todd's crotch, and closed her fingers around him. He was not fully erect yet, and when she squeezed him gently, she felt him swelling in response to her pressure.

"I'm thinking a lot, but no matter what I think, I'm not sure it's wise," she told him, her voice soft. "We can wait until tomorrow, when we get back to Baytown. We'd be a lot more comfortable in my room at the hotel."

"That's a long time to wait." Todd slid his hand into Jessie's blouse and groped for her breasts. She turned her body to make his search easier. He found his way under the camisole and his warm, work-firmed fingers began caressing her.

"At the spring, you said Dodds couldn't get here for three or four hours, didn't you?"

"Yes."

Jessie shuddered as she undid the buttons of his fly and freed his shaft. Todd was hard now, and Jessie felt herself melting in readiness for the time when she would feel the swollen flesh inside her.

"I don't care all that much for comfort," she said.

She unfastened the buttons of her skirt and slid it down to her knees, together with her brief pantalettes. Todd rolled above her and Jessie spread her legs as far as the hampering skirt would allow her. Holding his throbbing shaft, she rubbed its tip over the firm sensitive nubbin that was the center of all her sensation now, and moaned softly as the friction started her legs trembling.

Todd brought his hips down and his shaft slid from Jessie's hand and into the moist folds of flesh that were ready to receive it. Jessie rose to meet his thrust, and sighed as he began to stroke with quick hard jabs that ended in a rippling wave of sensation, setting her entire body quivering. Then, as Todd kept driving, Jessie sought his lips and for the first time they kissed fully, a twining of seeking, darting tongues that amplified the joyous trembling that swept her body each time Todd drove in.

"Go deeper, Todd!" she urged. "I want to feel you all the way inside me!"

"I can't, damn it! That skirt of yours is keeping you from lifting your hips high enough."

"Wait, then." Jessie pushed Todd away. He left her reluctantly and she felt empty and unsatisfied as the sensations she'd been enjoying rippled to a halt. Quickly she turned around, kneeling on knees and elbows, and thrust her buttocks high. "Now," she said urgently.

Kneeling behind her, holding her hipbones in his large hands, Todd drove hard and a whimper of satisfaction escaped Jessie's throat as he reached the end of his first deep lunge. She leaned forward, resting on her elbows, her buttocks reared, her thighs pulled together now to heighten the pleasure of Todd's driving penetrations. After weeks of continence, Jessie was more than ready when she swept into the small orgasm that always preceded the greater spasm that would follow. If Todd noticed that her body shook and if he heard her happy moaning, he paid no attention, but kept pounding in.

Jessie did not try to delay her second spasm or to restrain Todd's. She knew that she would deprive both herself and Todd of some of the pleasure they'd get by prolonging the time they were together, but promised herself that there would be a next time when they would not be concerned with what others were doing and could devote their full attention to their shared delights.

She let Todd carry her with him as he began gasping and speeding the tempo of his thrusts. When his hands tightened on her hips and his lunging reached the frantic point of no return, Jessie was with him, beginning to writhe in her own spasm. When Todd cried out breathlessly and clutched her even harder and pulled her buttocks against him and held her motionless while he poured himself into her, Jessie's

179

sensations were peaking too. She stiffened and quivered and her moans of ecstasy mingled with his until they were both spent and relaxed and Todd released her with a final sigh of satisfaction.

They lay side by side again, the night dark around them, and through the gloom Todd said, "I've stood watch a lot of times, Jessie, but I never did stand one I enjoyed so much."

"We'll enjoy our next time together even more," Jessie assured him. "Then, we won't have to worry about anything but ourselves."

"If you're tired and want to sleep, go ahead," Todd offered. "I'll rouse you if I feel like I'm about to drop off."

"That's a nice idea, Todd. I think I will doze a little while. If we trade off, watching and sleeping, the night won't seem so long."

Jessie curled up in Todd's arms and was asleep in a moment.

After Jessie and Todd left the spring, Ki looked at the Chinese women, who were sitting around the spring, washing and redoing their long hair. He told Darcy, "I suppose we'd better get Lan Ling and her friends busy making beds. I'll lend them my knife to cut the branches."

"Yes, the ground's a little bit hard for us to sleep on comfortably."

"Before I give them my knife, though," Ki went on, "I want to find a nice straight sapling and make myself a *bo*."

"What on earth is that?"

"It's the only weapon I can improvise from the material I see around here."

"Does it have something to do with *te?*"

"No. You don't use weapons with *te*, Darcy, just your hands. But a *bo* is very simple, just a straight stick."

180

"Oh. You mean a club."

"No, Darcy. Any lout can use a club. A *bo* is—well, come along and I'll show you."

Ki inspected the firs that grew thickly around the spring until he found a perfectly straight sapling of the proper length. He cut it off, and after he'd trimmed away the branches and bark, he used his knifeblade as a scraper to give its surface a smooth finish. Darcy watched him with perplexed interest.

"It's just a long club, like I said," she frowned when he'd finished trimming and smoothing the sapling.

"Quite a lot more than a club," Ki told her. He found a branch and quickly trimmed it to resemble a sword. "Here. Use this like a sword and stab me with it."

Still not quite understanding, Darcy thrust the point of the branch at Ki. He parried it easily and carried the opposite end of the *bo* around in a blow that would have struck Darcy's temple if he had not stopped it before impact. Her eyes widened.

"You could have killed me!" she exclaimed.

"Of course. Now try cutting like a sword, like you want to split my head open."

Again, Ki blocked Darcy's mock weapon with the improvised *bo*. This time he carried the end of the *bo* through in one smooth sweep, turning the block into an upward strike that brought the tip of the *bo* into Darcy's stomach.

"Your *bo* would be fine against a man with a sword, Ki. It wouldn't be much use against a gun, though," she objected.

"No. It was never intended to be. But if I hide by the trail and catch Dodds's men by surpise, I can do a lot of damage before they start shooting."

"It looks so simple to use, I think I could learn how."

"You can. Not the fine points, but the two or three basic *ute* and *ate* moves."

Darcy said thoughtfully, "Ki. If a *bo* is that easy to make and use, why couldn't you teach Lan Ling and her friends to use one? Then they could—"

"Hide along the trail and jump Dodds's men when they're not expecting to be attacked," Ki finished. "Of course I could. And will. There's still some daylight left. Let's get busy!"

Jessie was on watch and Todd was sleeping when Dodds's men came down the trail. Dawn had come, but the sun had not yet risen. Dodds and his gunmen made no effort to move quietly, and Jessie heard them coming long before they'd reached the stretch of bare rock. She woke Todd. He sat up, rubbing his eyes.

"They're coming, Todd."

"How many?"

"I couldn't see them, but if you'll listen—"

Todd concentrated on the noises drifting through the quiet air and nodded. "Ten or a dozen, from the noise they're making. And all of them armed, I'm sure. Let's go, Jessie. We'll get to the spring in plenty of time to scramble down to the boat. By the time they get there, we'll be rowing back to Fogarty's Bay."

They hurried back along the trail to the spring. Several minutes before they reached the clearing they heard Ki's voice, but could make no sense of what he was saying.

"Why are they making so much noise?" Jessie frowned. "All they're doing is making it easy for Dodds's thugs to locate us."

At the edge of the clearing, Jessie and Todd stopped short and gazed with amazement at the spectacle that met their eyes.

Ki was standing in front of the Chinese women, who formed a rough semicircle around him. Each of them held a peeled sapling about five feet long. Ki was demonstrating

182

the use of the *bo,* with Darcy as his foil. Lan Ling stood off to one side, translating Ki's instructions.

"What the hell's going on?" Todd asked.

Ki turned, and when he saw Jessie and Todd, his expression of total concentration became a smile.

"From the way you're hurrying, Dodds and his crew must be on the way," he said. "I'd like to have had more time to get my army ready for them, but we'll give them a surprise, anyhow. That's what will count."

"You're not planning to fight Dodds's gunmen with—" Todd asked incredulously, indicating the women. "Why, they'll cut you down with their first shots!"

"If my plan works, they won't fire those first shots," Ki said confidently. "They won't know what's happened to them until it's too late. We'll jump them as they come down the trail, and before they can fire a shot we'll have beaten them."

"Don't be a fool, Ki!" Todd urged. "We've got time to get down to the boat. We can make it back to Baytown before Dodds realizes we're gone, and rouse out enough men who used to work at Jessie's mill, and give Dodds a real fight!"

"Wait, Todd!" Jessie said. "Ki's plan may look foolish, but I've seen him bring off other plans that I've thought were crazy. It's got a chance of working. If it does, we'll end this thing right here, and without bloodshed."

Todd looked at the women with their improvised *bo*s. He sighed and shrugged as he said, "I guess you're the boss, Jessie, since we're not aboard my ship. All right, Ki. What do you want me to do?"

Dodds had quieted his men down as they drew closer to the spring, but when they entered the heavily wooded spot Ki had chosen for the ambush, they were still talking and laughing. All of them carried rifles; some held them in one hand, dangling at their sides, and others had their rifle butts tucked into an armpit with the barrel supported in the crook of their elbows.

With Dodds in the lead, they walked in single file, strung out along the narrow trail. Their feet scraped noisily as they plodded over the hard soil. The sun was just sending its bright rays through the tops of the tall firs, but the trail was still bathed in gloomy semidarkness.

Ki signaled the attack by leaping from behind the bole of the big fir where he was hidden. He landed with outspread feet in the trail in front of Dodds and loosed a loud shout to bring the women from similar hiding places as he felled Dodds with a *yoko ate* blow before he could draw his revolver.

Along the trail, the Chinese women had leaped out in similar fashion, and for a few brief seconds the still morning air was broken by the screams of the women and the solid thudding of blows landing, punctuated now and then by a sharper *thwack* as an improvised *bo* struck a rifle butt.

In ten seconds the battle had been fought and won. Dodds and his men were on the ground, kneeling with upraised arms or still lying unconscious from an accurate *bo* strike to the head. The Chinese women stood over them, threatening them with their own guns, which they'd scooped up. Darcy was moving along the line, taking revolvers from the plug-uglies.

Staring with disbelief, Todd shook his head and said, "I wouldn't have believed it if I hadn't seen it. Ki, maybe you'd take time to show me how to use one of those sticks before you and Jessie leave here."

"Ki won't have time," Darcy said quickly. "He's going to be busy giving me more *te* lessons."

"We won't be leaving soon anyhow," Jessie told Todd. "We'll have to get word to the capital to send somebody over to take Dodds to trial. And I've got to make plans for rebuilding the Starbuck mill." She paused while Todd looked at her with a small worried frown, and then added, "Oh, yes. You and I still have some unfinished matters to attend to as well, don't we, Todd? Don't worry. We'll have plenty of time to take care of them, too."

Watch for

Lone Star and the Showdowners

eighth in the hot new LONE STAR series from Jove

coming in February!